HOMETOWN HEARTLESS

CARRIE AARONS

For my hometown. Thank you for the heartbreak, the memories, the happiness and everything you taught me.

Do you want your **FREE** Carrie Aarons eBook?

All you have to do is **sign up for my newsletter**, and you'll immediately receive your free book!

1

My orange and white cheerleading skirt spills over my thighs and onto the driver's seat of my Jeep Wrangler.

In the passenger seat next to me, my pom-poms ruffle with every gust of wind that blows through the car. As does my hair, which I shouldn't even have bothered tying back in a ponytail. I'm eating chunks of my long chocolate locks, but it's worth it to keep the doors off my truck until it's so cold I'm forced to put them back on.

Khalid's voice bumps through my speakers as I hang a right, my pom-poms coming dangerously close to falling onto the street below. Indigo Drive comes into view in all of its picturesque glory. It's almost like the street I grew up on is *trying* to boast it's all-American, tree-lined, white picket fence, well ... street cred, for lack of a better word. When I was growing up on Indigo, there was a dog in every other yard, kids riding bikes until dusk, block parties; you name the Stepford suburb activity and our street had it. Each house includes some red brick in its design, sports an ample lawn that isn't *too* close to the neighbor's yard, and a range of expensive flowers dotting the front walk. My parent's even put in a porch swing to add curb appeal.

Although, let's not get too judgmental on clichés. I am the captain of the cheerleading squad who just ended her first day of senior year by sitting on the hood of her truck with her friends in the parking lot before cheer practice because it's the first year we've been allowed to drive to school and congregate after the final bell.

As I slow my speed, one of the newer mothers on the street swings a glare my way as her baby wails in her arms. Whatever, I lived here first. And it's only three p.m., I'm allowed to turn my car speakers to the max. It's practically a teenage rule of law.

Why are there so many people on the sidewalk? I wonder idly as my hands turn the wheel skillfully and practiced into the driveway of number nine Indigo Drive.

Grabbing my black backpack, with its Brentwick High School logo stamped on the front pocket, in one hand and my pom-poms in the other, I hop out of the truck. After a long day of school, the expectations of teachers, running cheer practice on my own, and already feeling the pressure of the college application process, I could use a snack. And maybe a nap. But I have homework, *on the first freaking day*, and my best friends want to grab sodas at the diner. Since my curfew has been extended to midnight, even on a school night, I better make the most of the last year in my hometown before college.

"Kennedy! *Oh*, Kennedy. They found him! He's *alive*."

Right before my mother's body slams into mine, I can see the rivulets of tears running down her face. She looks mad, like she's on the brink of a psychotic episode, and I'm so confused as she sobs into my shoulder.

I'm a carbon copy of this woman, same height, same brown hair, same big brown eyes. She blushes when strangers in public ask if she's my older sister. It just makes me glower, though I love her to the moon and back.

"What? What are you doing?" I try to push her back, because I genuinely have no idea what she's talking about.

Mom hiccups, sucking in a lungful, and a stinging awareness passes through me right before she opens her mouth. The words she just spoke finally penetrate my brain, soaking into the nerve endings and cortexes and all the tissue that is there to help you process, well, everything.

He's *alive*.

"Everett, honey. They rescued him. He's alive. *Oh, thank God.* Marcia and Grady got the call two hours ago, that he was on US soil. He's coming home. Everett is coming home."

Have you ever been so shocked that all you can do is laugh? It's a morbid reaction to emotional news, especially horrible news. Not that this is horrible news, this is incredible news. But I've always been one of those people who cackles hysterically in high-pressure, sad, emotionally charged, or otherwise situations. It's a defense mechanism, like my soul can't take the seriousness of the matter so it revolts against societal norms.

Well, my tried and true behavioral technique doesn't fail me now. While the rest of the neighborhood stands on the street crying tears of joy and weeping with relief, I double over, spill my pom-poms on the driveway, and laugh my goddamn head off.

"He's … coming … home." I giggle, holding my hand over my mouth to make it appear like I'm crying.

"Oh, Kennedy, not now!" Mom scolds, chiding me.

As if I can help this. I want to roll my eyes at her, but I'm too caught up in my fit of chuckling to do so.

It's comical, if you think about it. For an entire year, I've mourned the death of the boy I've dreamed about since I was old enough to have crushes. Laughter is the only way to react to the news that the prisoner of war, the hometown hero the entire town wept over, is coming home. That he's alive.

Everett Brock. And just like that, my memory jumps back two years' time, to the last time those bright green eyes held mine.

The rumbling of the truck coming down the street is unmistakable. No ordinary car sounds like that. It isn't the sleek, black car of death that visited the house next door just nine short months ago. That vehicle had been silent and vicious in its attack on our street.

No, this one announces its presence, causing everyone on the street to whip their heads toward it.

I make out the camouflage paint on the old Ford pickup before I even realize that it's headed straight for me. Everything feels like a dream right now, as if my life is moving in slow motion but my heartbeat has settled somewhere between manic and atrial fibrillation.

I straighten, my mouth sobering to the point that not only will laughter not come out, I'm not even sure breath is escaping past my lips.

He's in there, I know it. Why else would an army vehicle from the base about an hour from here be driving down the street we both grew up on?

"Oh my Lord ..." Mom gasps, because everyone is watching this like some kind of car crash they can't look away from.

None of us have any idea what he might look like.

A car is fast on the truck's tail, and this one I would know anywhere. Marcia and Grady Brock come screeching around the corner in their navy blue BMW, and the car slams into park on the street. They're out in a flash, dashing across the driveway, and Marcia sends a watery smile Mom's way.

The door to the truck opens in the driveway next door, an officer pulling the handle.

I see a boot first, black, scuffed. Part of me wants to look away, wants to wait until he's fully out of the car. I'm not sure I can handle it bit by bit, or if seeing him full-on for the first time in two years will be worse.

But I am helpless at this point. I wish I could stop time, have a minute or two more to process this.

A long leg follows it, and then another, and then he's appearing from the truck as if he hasn't risen from the dead.

No longer the boy I waved goodbye to as he drove off to basic training, Everett stands before me in the body of a man. Ropey muscles coat his arms, the height I thought he possessed before now put to shame by the couple extra inches he miraculously sprouted since eighteen. A scruffy beard masks most of his face, and his hair is too long and greasy, but anyone can see how intensely handsome he is, even under the coarse forest.

It's one of those moments in life, when you look back on it, that will be set to music in the memory. As my eyes trail up, hitting every part of his long, lean body, a sorrow-filled, haunting melody plays in my ears. The kind of tune that departing lovers dance to before they're separated. A harmony with only one note of hope thrown in at the end, only a singular note of uplift.

I swear, I almost lose my balance when my face is level to his.

Because there are dozens of people on the street now. His parents are practically sobbing over him. My own mother is calling his name, yelling her congratulations. The army officers are murmuring to him, and I hear the slamming of doors as I know that local reporters must have rushed to get the news on the missing hero who has just returned.

But Everett is only looking at me.

The whole world might as well have vanished, that's how soul-deep his exploration of me is. My feet are rooted to the ground, every cell in my body completely paralyzed by the direct, *familiar* gaze he's pinned on me.

I look at him, trying to memorize every pore. Yes, he resembles the boy who left to serve his country. But this *man* is no one I truly recognize.

And those eyes, the blazing green clovers that I've daydreamed about for years, are ... dead. In them, I see only ghosts and horror.

Everett Brock is back in Brentwick. And nothing will ever be the same.

2

KENNEDY

"*He's back.*"

"*Did you hear how he came back?*"

"*I wonder if he was tortured ...*"

"*Is he some kind of maniac now?*"

The whispering in the hallways as the first bell rings for homeroom is almost too much for me to handle.

I slam my locker, biting my tongue because if I don't, I might lose it on all of these people. No one here really knows him, not like I do. Jesus, half of these freshman have never even seen Everett Brock in the flesh, so maybe they should just shut their mouths.

"Already fed up with school a week in? Me too, let's ditch." A flash of red hair sidles up next to my locker, accompanying the voice that leads the Brentwick High School choir.

"Yeah, right, Kenny would never ditch. She'd melt into a puddle of guilt and shame before she walked out of those doors before the final bell rung."

My two best friends, Rachel and Bianca, stand on either side of my white metal locker, staring into the abyss filled with books, extra clothes, a stray granola bar somewhere and pictures of the three of us littering the door.

"That's right, get a good laugh at the expense of your very dear, wonderful, incredible friend." I pretend to wipe away a tear.

"Oh, stop it. We're just busting your balls. Because we know you have them. You may be the goody two-shoes of BHS, but you've got steel cojones under that skirt." Rachel pretends to flip up the hem of the denim skirt I wore today.

I swat her hand away. "Don't you dare!"

"Live a little. I showed my undies to a boy in the bathroom this morning, and it really brightened my day." Bianca suggestively wiggles her dirty blond eyebrows at me.

I roll my eyes. "That boy is your boyfriend, and I still don't understand why you two can't just go at it in your cars if you insist on foreplay before first period. Nonetheless, that doesn't quite count as randomly flashing the student body in the hallway."

"Foreplay before first period. Sounds like a great porn movie." Rachel giggles.

These two have been my best friends since the time we all decided to shove tampons up our noses at cheer practice in fifth grade. Someone told Rachel it would stop the bloody nose that were sometimes caused when we flew, the thing cheerleaders did when other members of the squad launch them into the air using nothing but their collective hands. So, giggling like morons, we tried it. And took about seventy-three hilarious selfies, one of which is still hung up on the inside of my locker.

Ever since that moment, we've been inseparable, though we all play our roles. Rachel is the wild child, the redhead who isn't afraid to tell it like it is, or try something that could potentially end with us in the emergency room. Though, she is the one with the longest relationship, she and her boyfriend, Scott, have been together since the beginning of sophomore year. The contradiction, of her big, open heart, and the daredevil within, makes being friends with her like an extreme sport. One I thoroughly enjoy, though aside from cheer, I'm not much of an athlete.

Bianca is the sweet one, a natural charmer with Disney princess-sized blue eyes and gorgeous blond curls. She's the extrovert of us all; whereas I don't mind interaction but prefer quiet, and Rachel is an obnoxiously loud introvert, Bianca could talk her way through a football field of people and genuinely never have one mean thing to say. Then, she'd ask to do it all over again. Rach and I always joke that after she graduates college, she'll be some kind of social worker, customer service rep, or salesperson; Bianca will work in a job where rejection is copious and other people would cower at the mere thought of their ass being handed to them by whoever they were serving. But not our Bianca.

She's also dating a fellow senior, Damien, who shares her affinity for public hookup spots.

"Get your mind out of the gutter." I cluck my tongue at her, but loop my arm through hers as we all walk toward our homerooms.

And me? Well, my best friends already hit that nail on the head. I'm the straight-laced, academic one. The nerd.

Brentwick High School is much like any other high school in the suburbs of New Jersey. Or any other suburb around the country for that matter. You have your rich side of town, your nice middle of town, and the affordable housing units the township was contracted to build due to state law. Not that I roll like that; I have friends from all walks of life. I'm just saying, that's how it is.

I may be the head cheerleader, if you want to call me that, but I'm also an honor student, an EMT on the local rescue squad, and have been volunteering with my mom at our local church since I was in middle school. No, I'm not trying to brag or sound like a goody-goody ... okay, so maybe I *am* a goody-goody according to Rach and Bi. In fact, if you talk to some of the kids at school, they'll probably sneer and call me some uptight perfectionist or something.

That's all right. I know who I am, have from an early age. Maybe it's the side effect of being an only child with a type A personality, or parents who instilled self-confidence in me. Either way, I've developed some kind of Teflon armor when it comes to how cruel the high school world can be. Something I'm both thankful for and cursed with.

Sometimes, I wish I could be more of a teenager. My dad swears that I've been an old soul since I arrived in the world, blinking up at the doctors with a wise look on my face instead of crying. While my friends are mooning over boys, drinking warm beer in cornfields, and generally being reckless and eighteen, I'm standing in the background wondering why I can't do the same. Something inside has always held me back from completely letting go, from letting mistakes happen, from letting the crazy take over.

"It's permanently stuck there, I can't help it. Someone has to think of questions to shock you when we're playing Never Have I Ever. Who else could make you chug an entire can of beer in one sitting." Rachel gleams proudly.

"Oh my God, that was amazing. Can we do that again this weekend? Party at the tree house!" Bianca claps her hands as if it's not eight a.m. on a Tuesday.

"Yes! I'll tell the whole crew. We'll go after the football game. Do you think your cousin can get us a keg?" Rachel turns to me.

"I can't ask for that again." I shake my head, almost stomping my foot to show them just how down it is.

Crap, I should not have done that for the last party we had right before the school year. I knew it would come back to bite me in the ass. While I'm not the "let's do ten shots and get buck naked" kind of party girl, I can let my hair down and have a good time. So, when Scott couldn't come through with his alcohol supply for the end of summer barn party the seniors threw, I called in a favor to my cousin. She lives a town over, is twenty-one, and has offered to buy me whatever I want a number of times.

I've never taken her up on it until that one time, and I knew my friends would expect this alcohol source to continue. After all, it's not easy for high schoolers to get liquor on demand. But isn't it funny how we always find a way?

"Okay, we can talk about it later. Gotta run!" Rachel bull-dozes over my protests.

"But, I—"

"Love you, Kenny!" Bianca hums my nickname.

I clamp my lips shut, because there is no point in arguing. And it's all teasing anyway, no harm in it.

Unfortunately, we're all in separate homerooms, so it's high fives, hugs, and goodbyes for us until lunch. I'm in mostly advanced classes, as is Rachel, but Bianca decided to sprinkle her senior schedule with more electives than academic courses.

But, we did all get put into the same lunch period, which is amazing. Finally being allowed to sit in the senior courtyard is pretty damn exclusive, if you ask me. In reality, it's just a bunch of picnic tables right outside the cafeteria doors that only seniors are allowed to occupy. Though we treat it like the Buckingham Palace gardens.

As I walk into homeroom though, my mind shifts to *him*. Of course, it does. I haven't been able to go the last twenty-four hours since he stepped out of that truck without thinking of Everett Brock every other minute.

I'm honestly surprised Rachel and Bianca haven't broached the subject, but maybe they're giving me time to come to them.

After all, I had a bit of a meltdown when the military came to tell us he was dead. A meltdown is putting it lightly. I had to take almost a month's leave from school, I could barely get it together.

Two years ago, Everett left for basic training. He was deployed as a Marine some couple of months after that, though his letters never contained specific details because he wasn't allowed to disclose them. I estimate that around six months into his deployment; again, I have no specifics to back this up, he was taken by the enemy as a prisoner of war. That term comes from the officers who contacted Marcia, his mother. She had told my mother this at the table in our breakfast nook, and I was eavesdropping on the stairs.

Right then, I'd dropped to my knees and prayed on the top step. For God to bring him home. For Everett to be strong through whatever he was going through. My nightmares were things of blood and horror, thinking about what he must be enduring. For three months we hoped, held the vigils, wrote letters to the military, and tried to be positive.

Then, the black car of death arrived, with government officials claiming to believe they had sufficient evidence proving Everett's death. They handed his mother a folded American flag and promptly went on their way.

I remember the day of his funeral, almost the entire town of Brentwick standing in the cemetery. It was a sea of black, sobs coming from every which direction. When they lowered the empty casket, the shots rang out—the military had arranged for a twenty-one gun salute. I jumped at every single bullet fired, as if they were all being riddled right through my heart.

This was the boy I thought I'd marry someday. Not that we'd ever dated, or had any moments that crossed over into the territory of more than friends. It was more of a feeling. A larger sense of fate's plan in the grand scheme of things. Everett and I had danced around each other since we were children, teetering on the edge of becoming something more for the years we were in high school together.

I'd even been so bold as to ask him a few times, when I was tipsy and he couldn't help but plant me in his lap at a party, why he'd never made a move. We'd sit there at the barn, our friends surrounding us, and he'd tap me on my nose while his other hand played with the hem of my shirt. Usually, he'd brush me off, say something about being friends or that I was his kid sister. Which inevitably shattered my heart and caused a mess of drunk tears by the time we arrived at one of two best friend's basements to sleep off the alcohol.

And then, on the last night before he shipped out to boot camp, we found ourselves in the same position. Anyone who saw the way he held me, or saw the way I looked at him ... they knew it was much more than a friendly gesture. So I asked him to kiss me. To give me my first kiss, the one I'd been holding out for.

"It's not our time, yet, Kennedy. Plus, you're still too young. I'm going away, and you're going to live your life here. But when you turn eighteen, I'm going to come back for you. And I'm going to give you the kiss we've both dreamed about. Wait for me."

I always used to love that he insisted on using my full name when everyone else shortened it to Kenny.

Of course, the sophomore me who had drunk two wine coolers that night hadn't understood why he couldn't just kiss me right there on the spot. It had annoyed me, frustrated me. So much so that I didn't write to him for the first four weeks, because I was sulking at his trying to teach me patience.

But over time, I had to admit that what Everett had proposed was poetic. He was right, in a way. I hadn't known then what I thought I did. I wasn't ready. It wasn't our time.

Though, once he was captured, and eventually pronounced

a casualty of war, I thought we would never have our time. I'd waited for him, and he'd died.

Now, he's back, and everyone in my high school is talking about it. It's all I can think about.

Well, that and the kiss he owes me. I just keep wondering if he'll ever make good on his promise.

3

I 'm back from the dead, motherfuckers.

Well, I guess not the dead. The seventh circle of hell is more like it, though at that point, you just wish you were dead.

I suppose I actually am. At least that's how everyone keeps looking at me, like they're utterly shocked to see my skin and hair where they assumed there would be rotting bone and dead eyes. I don't have the energy to tell them that's how I feel on the inside.

Do you want to break a person? Toss them in a four foot by eight foot hole for three hundred and sixty-five days, starve them, beat them within an inch of their life, and then throw away the key. That'll get the job done.

How do you just pick up a life that is no longer anything resembling that? Normal people leave the house, have friends, smile, enjoy aspects of the living, breathing world around them. I can no longer do those things. It's like the enemy sliced into my chest with their box of tools and removed the part of me that can feel anything. I bet if you took a scalpel to my leg, gutted the

thing wide open like the belly of a fish, I'd feel absolutely
nothing.

My mom and dad have been tiptoeing around me. Their not-
so-subtle check-in's, since I won't come out of my room; the
pretend pass by with a bit of food on a tray, the questions about
taking my car out of storage, the book on PTSD they just
happened to pick up for me. They're probably elated to have
their son back, after he was buried in the local cemetery, but I
just can't muster up any kind of emotion for them.

Sure, they're my parents. I recognize that they're a safe place,
though what that means to me anymore is completely fucked.
But I can't muster the spirit to sit at a dinner table with them. To
even crack a small smile when my mother tells me how much
she's missed me. And don't even think about asking me to detail
the events of the last year of my life. If I did that, they'd be stabbing themselves in the ears to stop my words from entering
them, that's how brutal the stories I could tell are.

No, there is only one random, annoying as hell, uncontrol-
lable thought that keeps running through my mind.

When I shipped out, Kennedy Dover was a sophomore
who'd just gotten her braces removed. Of course, neither of
those two things kept me from wanting her. Fuck, I'd wanted her
even when she had the braces. Kennedy has always been
gorgeous, even as the girl who used to knock my sand castle over
in the park sandbox. One doesn't need to guess why she was my
first crush, and my pen pal as I sat in a fucking desert trying not
to be shot at.

Kennedy encompasses all ends of the spectrum when it
comes to beauty. She has the obvious, pretty vibe with the long
lashes that kiss her cheeks when she blinks. All the swirling
brown hair that you can't help but want to touch. The button
nose and pure white teeth, sans braces. Not only that, but she's
sexy as hell and has no idea, which only makes her sexier. Even

back then, before I left, she was starting to fill into her curves. A petite frame with a handful of tit on each side, an ass made perkier by all the cheerleading jumps and stunts, and legs longer than the afternoon in summer. It was all I could do to stop staring at her lips before I graduated high school, so full they are, and the color of crushed cherries. Kennedy has always been beautiful, a natural kind of attractiveness that goes further than just skin deep. She's considerate and polite, sincerely cares and gives her attention when she's having a conversation with you. She has that spark, the one that draws people to her.

That was before. Before I turned into a ghost of my former self. But now? *Jesus fucking Christ.* It took all I had in me not to tackle her like a wild animal when I stepped into my driveway and saw her standing there. She's a goddamn knockout, all supple curves in that tight cheer uniform. She's every guy's wet dream come to life.

From the moment I saw her standing across the lawn that separates our two houses, she's been the only thing that can penetrate the fortress that is now my mind. Being by myself, in a dusty pit with not a speck of light, it trained me to focus my mind into a full meditative state. I can go weeks without having a single thought.

But since the second I saw Kennedy Dover, I haven't been able to stop thinking about the last thing I said to her in person.

"I'm going to give you the kiss we've both dreamed about. Wait for me."

That fucking promise I made her, the one about the kiss? It was what got me through the first few months of fighting overseas. Before I got captured, all I did was eat, sleep, shoot, and read Kennedy's letters. We would send them back and forth so frequently, sometimes I'd get random handwritten pages that didn't even correspond to the letter I'd just sent because she'd already sent another one.

They were always about everything, and nothing at all. The scrawl of her penmanship kept me grounded, kept me sane even as I stared at the same orange desert landscape for hours on end. Fuck, I can still feel the grit of that sand in my eyes even now, and I was rescued over a month ago from the pit those fucking bastards left me in.

Took the guys who are supposed to be on my side long enough to realize I was telling the truth when I said I hadn't been turned. That I wasn't a spy for the other team, that no one had radicalized me. When they were satisfied—after using their own methods of psychological torture because apparently I haven't had enough—I was given a Prisoner of War medal and a Purple Heart, allowed to go into surgery for my fucked up arm and leg, and shipped home. A simple nod of their heads to thank me for my service, as if I wasn't just tortured and dragged through hell. No talk of the benefits I'd receive, or if I'd have some kind of exit discussion. No HR rep calling my line in the past few days.

When I turned eighteen, I did the noble thing and decided to serve my country. And now, that country was abandoning me.

But at least I kept the one secret that no one was able to pull out of me. Maybe because they didn't know it was there, locked tightly in my brain, where no one could unveil it. Because they would never believe an eighteen-year-old kid could pull it off.

Shipping me back to Brentwick, a white-picket town where high school football heroes are held up as nobility, and the Christmas Eve parade is the most anticipated event on the calendar. My hometown was untouchable in my mind as a teenager. The two-story brick home my parents own, the late-night parties on the acres of farm property my best friend lives on, victory laps when the football team won ... it all adds to the nostalgic charm that my northern New Jersey hometown is known for. I grew up as an only child, riding my bike down to Brentwick's main street, Dellan Drive, and playing T-ball at the municipal fields.

To most, my upbringing probably seems idyllic. I was lauded as a golden boy, and what did I do? Decided to follow my hero worship with an inflated ego and cocky heart right onto the battlefield. What a fucking moron I was.

And now, I'm a twenty-year-old veteran with pins holding my ankle together after some Iraqi army general smashed it with a ball peen hammer, no job since I can't seem to leave my room without hearing fucking helicopter blades coming for me, and no real will to live.

Staring up at the white, wood-paneled ceiling of my childhood bedroom, I'm still truly shocked whenever I observe the space. Mom and Dad touched nothing, as if they were leaving it an intact shrine. Maybe they really did know I'd come home at some point, because nothing has changed. My little league baseball and football trophies still sit on a shelf above my desk. On that dark wood desk, where I used to hide a Playboy Magazine in the bottom drawer under old action figures, sit my senior year textbooks. The orange and white football jersey from my junior year state championship win, the one Mom had framed, hangs on the wall above my queen-sized bed. A wall of built-in bookcases covering the entire length of the wall opposite the door contains my favorite science-fiction novels, old CDs from my childhood days, wood shop projects, framed pictures of my friends, and a couple of priceless sports memorabilia I'd received as Christmas presents. I used to think the football signed by Brett Favre was the most valuable thing I own. Now, I could care less about the fucking pigskin.

Aside from the last thing I said to Kennedy, I can think of nothing else I truly want to do. But this morning, my mom left a note on my desk before she left for work. *Please go outside. Walk, or sit in the backyard, but you need some fresh air.*

If she only knew about the brutal heat I'd sat in for a little under a year, in that fucking hole in the desert, then she wouldn't be saying it.

But, I haven't got anything else to do. And if I have to listen to the silence ringing in my head for one more minute, I might have a full-blown PTSD attack.

So I drag myself from the bed, throw a pair of sneakers on, and go outside.

4

KENNEDY

The air smells of autumn when I step out of my car onto the driveway.

Most people wouldn't agree, what with it being nearly eighty degrees and my tank top and short skirt demonstrating otherwise. But, I can tell. Each September, there is a certain day where the weather gives you a clue that it's about to change. That the leaves will change color brilliantly soon, that you'll have to pull your sweaters out, that the pumpkin spice everything will flock to your local grocery shelves and coffee counters.

Right now is that time, and I almost can't wait for it. Mostly, because I love New Jersey in the fall, and partly because I'm sick of my summer wardrobe and can't wait to break out my boots.

Though, the fall only makes the elephant's weight worth of pressure sitting on my shoulders that much more apparent.

My head is not swirling with Bi and Rachel's weekend plans. Though, not for their lack of trying. My best friends love to discuss party plans for the weekend before the present weekend is even over. And I like it enough. I'm always up for a party, to hang around, to try to relax.

But I'm me. I have my eyes on some sort of prize, always.

And right now, that prize is college. And that elephant on my back? He's aware that the first signs of fall mean one step closer to applications being due.

I'm gunning for my dream school, with my dream nursing program. I've known that I wanted to be a nurse since I was, oh, seven maybe? The first time I realized I didn't get squeamish around blood, but ran to help at the sight of Rachel's bone sticking out of her arm after a cheerleading stunt gone bad ... yeah, I think that's probably when I knew for sure. What other profession combines the complex knowledge and challenge of medicine, with the art of caring, and mental and physical toughness put on a nurse each day? It's the perfect career for me.

The perfect school is about two hours from here, with a top-notch, elite nursing program. Follow that with a two-year master's program to become a nurse practitioner, and I will have accomplished everything that is stressing me out to the max right now.

Yes, I have a five-year plan. And a ten-year plan. And if you ask me what my twenty-year plan is, I could probably tell you that, too. Call me a psycho, that's fine. I'm motivated and determined, which are two of the least damaging vices if you ask me.

College essay writing hasn't been going all that well, mainly because ... I can't dig deep enough into something to make it sound sincere. I'm a white cheerleader from an upper-middle class tri-state town, who is an only child and has never really had to compete for anything in her life. To universities, I'm just one face in a million. When I sit down to write, I'm suddenly struck by how much all the groups, clubs, charity drives, and activities I only participated in so I could put them on my college résumé ... well, how much they really don't matter. I've never had or done one thing in my life because I was simply following my heart.

My eyes redirect to the second-story window of the house next to mine. The one I've stared at countless nights in the dark as a pre-teen girl, wondering if the boy inside was thinking about me too. Everett's window has always faced mine, the alleyway between our homes always representing more than just a patch of lawn in distance. He was my childhood crush, the one that grew into unrequited love. When we all thought he was gone, I took those feelings and stuffed them deep down, in a dark, hidden place.

I tried to get over them, tried to move on. For a while, it was working, even if I had to lie to myself.

And then I saw him, back from the dead.

I haven't glimpsed him except for his arrival in his driveway. Over the last four days, the curtains to his room have never moved, the light never flicked on in the nighttime hours. Everett hasn't ventured outside, and no one aside from his parents have come or gone from the house.

Watching the window, I will him to peek out, to do something. I have no idea what he might be feeling right now, but it's been killing me not to go over there and just ... look at him. Make sure it's real, make sure that he's actually alive and home.

I'm about to drop my head and walk through the garage entrance at the side of my house, when I notice movement out of the corner of my eye. My body stills as I realize ... it's him.

He's sitting in a chair on the patio out back, and I can just make him out at my vantage point. That's when I realize, he's been watching me this entire time.

Everett sits in a reclined, relaxed positioned, his hands folded in his lap over black jogger sweatpants, dog tags hanging out in the open against his gray long sleeve T-shirt. His biceps and pecs strain against the material, and I wonder what they look like underneath. How much has his physical body changed in the two years he's been gone?

When I make it up to his face, an errant lock of strawberry-blond hair dips onto his forehead. But it's the eyes that capture me like a deer in headlights. Those intense emeralds don't match his lazy posture at all; I've been caught looking for him, and he's either amused or angry. I can't decide which.

Without thought, I walk past the garage entrance, and follow the dividing line of our properties. My feet carry me to his backyard, up the stone patio steps, and straight in front of him where I stop.

The two of us stare at each for a beat, and I try to find any shred of the boy I once knew. He stands, towering over me, my eyes never leaving his even when I'm forced to crane my neck. It's like he's asserting his dominance, standing to his tallest height.

"Oh, *Everett*. I can't believe you're home."

All the emotions I've been holding inside since he left all those many months ago flood me, and I fling my arms around his neck. He still smells like he used to, like a rainy day in the forest, but underneath his plain ensemble, there are muscles that he didn't sport before. My body melts into his, that comfort I've sought for two years finally warming my skin like a favorite blanket. There is something more, too. A charged, electric current between us, and I'm surprised neither of us is shocked when we make contact. For two years, I've dreamed, fantasized, and mooned over how the boy next door would finally hold me. How he'd kiss me, just like he wrote in his last letter.

And then a split-second later, I'm being shoved off of him. I'm so surprised, I nearly topple over myself. Wobbling to regain balance, I take three steps away from him, my mouth falling open.

"Don't fucking touch me without my permission."

His voice could cut steel, that's how sharp and demanding it is. Those full plum lips smash into a furious straight line, his nostrils flaring like an agitated animal.

Of course. Jesus Christ, how could I be so *stupid*? Everett has been tortured for the better part of a year, in ways I can't even imagine. My mother thinks I didn't hear her talking in hushed tones to Marcia Brock in our living room the night of his return. Of course, he doesn't want someone to touch him unexpectedly.

"You're glad I'm home? Yeah, well, I'm fucking not. I wish I never had to step foot in Brentwick again. Why do you think I signed up for a job that has like a ninety percent chance of being shipped home in a body bag?"

His morbid words, the venom in his tone ... I had no idea who I was dealing with when I wished for a reunion with Everett.

And the only thought I can latch onto is that he never wanted to come back. I'm just heartbroken enough from this revelation, and just pissed off enough from the way he's speaking to me, that I let the words fall out of my mouth.

"So then, you never planned on kissing me the day I turned eighteen?"

The minute I say them, I want to shove them back in. I want to scoop them up in my arms, choke them down and get sick on those words. They're the most selfish, horrible syllables I could have said. Everett is dealing with years of psychological and physical trauma, he has every right to lash out and hurt those around him if it helps him feel better, and all I'm worried about is being given a kiss like some fairy-tale princess.

My cheeks are so red, I can feel the blush flame in them, that I begin to sweat. If I'm so embarrassed about this, then thank my lucky stars he never received one of the last letters I wrote. The worn envelope still sits in my desk, two stories above us, the words I never should have written thankfully, never seeing the light of day.

Everett's green eyes flash, and I watch a muscle in his jaw twitch. And then ... he grins.

It's not nice. It's not friendly or even teasing. No, this expression is full of piss and vinegar, a mean, rude upturn of his lips.

"God, you're so obsessed with yourself, aren't you, Kennedy? Desperate and stuck in your little high school bubble. The biggest dilemma on your mind is whether to sleep with the high school quarterback on prom night. You have no idea what the real world is like. It'll be like a bullet to your brain by the time you discover just how fucking cruel it is."

I don't even equate what he just said to me to a verbal smackdown. No, it's much worse. This kind of malevolence, of hate ... it comes from deep within the soul. Everett may not hate me specifically, but he loathes everything I stand for. According to him, he never wanted to see my face again.

My heart is so dejected as I turn to walk away, I'm convinced I'll have to glue it back together later. There is nothing like the devastating blow of a first crush gone wrong. Not to mention what Everett is to me. He made promises, wrote me things in letters that could rival the romance of Shakespeare. All of it just came crashing down on my head, splintering into so many pieces that I know I'll never be able to collect them all in hopes of repair.

Lead riddles my legs and feet as I turn, trying to hold the tears back until I'm safely on the other side of my garage door.

I'm almost safe, back across the distance of the lawn, when that deep voice rumbles.

"Hey, just for shits and giggles, did you wait for me?"

I have to turn; I know I have to. I'm the one who posed the question first, and the truth would have come out at some point. Guilt drowns my gut, even in the midst of the horrible things he just said to me. Facing him, I know he can read it all over my face.

Everett looks skyward, chuckling bitterly. "So, some other guy gave you that goddamn kiss? Way to hold out hope."

It's as if he's slapped me. My face burns with shame and the sting of his words.

I waited, I did. The entire year he was overseas, I waited. When they told us he was gone, it took almost six months for me to even agree to hang out with my friends on a weekend. And when another boy sat beside me, whispering sweet nothings at a party, I let him kiss me. I let that insignificant, meaningless boy take the thing Everett promised to give me. I'd been so upset afterward, that it took me weeks to stop feeling nauseous every time I thought about my first kiss.

And now I'm furious. He'd never planned to give me that kiss in the first place. He just insulted everything I hold dear about myself. How does he get the nerve to slut shame me? To accuse me of being in the wrong?

"What was I supposed to do? I waited for as long as I could. I thought you were dead!"

"I am *dead*!" he roars.

I take a few steps back, as if the sheer impact of his voice has the ability to knock me over.

A few of the tears I swore I wouldn't let fall end up trickling down my cheek, and I slap my hand to them.

The damage is done though. He's said the words and seen me breakdown because of them. What I thought would be a reunion for the ages, turned sour before I could even grasp it in my hands.

The only thing left to do is turn and flee before my heart shatters any further.

5

EVERETT

"Come on, buddy, you have to get dressed. You have therapy."

Mom's voice comes from somewhere above, the groggy cloud of drug-induced sleep lingering in my bones and mind.

It's the only way I can sleep these days, by swallowing enough pills that I eventually pass out. The military doctors gave them to me, and I stashed them in a box at the top of my closet where only I can find them. Better to take drugs like candy than talk about your problems ... or at least that's one of the lessons I learned about PTSD among military members.

Not only do the individual sufferers not want to address it, but it's easier for our superiors if all the mental strife is kept under wraps. Of course, the general public knows that currently serving soldiers and veterans are going to be fucked up by the things they experience. Even those in positions of non-direct combat, like doctors or photographers, come back with their brains jumbled. But the higher ups don't want that advertised. Silencing us with pills and the sense of manly solidarity is easier.

I don't mean to criticize the shit out of the organization I voluntarily decided to work for. Mind you, there are a ton of people I interacted with that had good morals, wanted to serve their country out of honor and duty, and who I consider brothers and sisters in arms. But it's the few douchebags that sour the bunch. The ones who want to sweep just how mentally fucked soldiers are under the rug, so that they can keep signing up eighteen-year-old kids to run into militant provinces. The ones who would have rather me died in that hole than bring me back and deal with the PR nightmare that my lack of being murdered causes. The ones who abuse the civilians we're supposed to be protecting from the terrorists in their country.

"Not going." I turn over, trying to will myself back into the cave of narcotics that threatens to pull me under.

"You have to. It's part of your discharge requirements. So, even if I can't force you, the military can." She clanks a belt and shoes down on my desk, having probably picked out an outfit for me.

I know me being home is wearing thin. It's been two weeks, and she's probably stunned to realize that her golden boy son is gone forever. In the first few days of my homecoming, it was all happy tears, hugs, my favorite food, and thanking God and the universe that they brought me home to them. As the shine wears off, and my parents are left with the fallout of the son that returned to them, I see my mom growing more and more frustrated.

I barely talk, barely eat, don't come out of my room, and refuse to do much of anything. Trying to get me to go to doctor's appointments is like pulling teeth, I know she wrinkles her nose at the smell every time she walks into my room, and generally, I'm just in a foul mood every second I'm awake. For Mom and Dad, it probably seems like life should go back to the way it was before I shipped out. Their miracle was granted, but it's nothing like they planned.

My parents weren't thrilled about my decision to sign up for the Marines. I was a mostly A and B student in high school, quarterback of the football team, bright, social, and could have had my pick of top-notch colleges in the area. I'd never really discussed my plans with them until I was halfway through the physical and mental examination process to enroll in basic training.

I remember the day I told them I was going to fight overseas. Mom burst into hysterics, clinging to my shirt like I'd just signed my death sentence. Dad had eyed me cautiously, like I might poof into thin air if he took his eye off of me for one second. In the end, he convinced my mother that they couldn't stop me, that what I was doing was noble, and hadn't they wanted to raise a noble man?

And then I'd betrayed my country. I'd done the one thing I wasn't supposed to do. Soldiers fell in line. I disobeyed that, and ended up in the wrong place, at the wrong time. What happened to me was my own fault, but I'd do it all over again.

"No one can force me to do anything. Not anymore," I tell her, throwing my trauma in her face.

These days, it's what I'm best at; obnoxiously pointing out all the shit I've endured so that I don't have to do whatever someone is trying to make me do.

Mom makes a sputtering noise. "Everett, that's not what I meant—"

I cut her off. "Of course, it wasn't. You'd never want to imply that someone who was tortured and forced to do things would be put through something like that again."

I'm a fucking dick, but I can't stop.

"Please, Everett, just let me take you to therapy. It can help you." Now there are tears in Mom's voice, and I'm not sure if it's because of the way I'm talking to her, or if she just wants her boy back.

Clearly, she's not going to leave me alone, and the smallest pang of guilt, the only amount I've felt in a year, flicks me in the gut. Grumbling, I push up off the mattress and grab the jeans she's laid out. Without saying anything, I start dressing, and she leaves.

Twenty minutes later, Mom pulls her car into a spot in front of your typical looking doctor's office. I'm not sure if my parents sold my truck, if they're hiding it so I can't leave the house on my own, or what, but I haven't been granted permission to drive anywhere yet. Nothing that makes you feel trapped more than having your parents drive your twenty-year-old ass around your hometown.

The building is a white-shingled rectangle spanning about half a football field, with red steel doors and a window cutout in the middle of each. The handle is a steel knob, and above each office suite is a number, with a gold plate located on the right side of the door, telling you which doctor is located inside.

Silence envelops us we get out of my mother's BMW and walk into the office marked "Dr. Janice Liu, Psychiatrist, M.D., D.O." After we check in with the receptionist, we sit, my mother filling out my paperwork. She doesn't even hand it to me, probably because she knows I won't complete it.

The lobby of Dr. Janice Liu's office is everything I envision a therapist's office to look like. Neutral, muted tones of decor, no loud TV in the corner but soothing nature sounds set to music playing over the speakers, and comfortable but professional couches and chairs arranged around a wooden coffee table.

The sound of a door being opened has my head snapping toward it, and a slim, decently attractive, Asian woman walks out of it. She's younger than my mom, but has that professional air about her that is supposed to convince her patients she's been doing this for a long time. This has to be Dr. Liu, who else would this be? Her long, midnight-black hair runs straight down her back, almost brushing her ass, which is unfortunately encased in wide, flowing khaki pants, so I can't make out the shape. Therapy wouldn't be so bad if I had something to ogle.

"Hello, Everett, Marcia." She smiles warmly, crossing the small lobby and extending a hand for my mother and I to shake, respectively.

"Thank you for seeing my son." My mom replies.

"Shall we get started? Everett, why don't you come into my office?" Dr. Liu's voice has this soothing but direct quality to it, and I find myself following her.

Her office is decorated in the same style as the lobby, though there are three large paintings of herbs hanging over the back of her desk. She takes a seat in the chair behind it, and motions for me to sit in a plush armchair kitty-corner to the glass desk separating us.

"I'm glad you came to see me today. Just walking in here is a good first step." She starts the conversation, and I can't read her, which only makes me more weary.

I don't like therapists. I don't like doctors who keep their cards close to the vest. Honestly, I don't like anyone who keeps their cards close. Before I flew into a war zone, I was one of the most honest guys I knew. There should be no tolerance for bullshit, omissions, and lying, in my opinion. But then my world was flipped on its head, and I began to really see the true colors people were hiding.

My silence is answer enough for Dr. Liu, because she gives me a slight smile, and tries again.

"In here, everything you say is confidential. We can talk

about your time overseas, your torture, the thoughts you're experiencing now. Anything you want to disclose, stays between us."

Quiet chirps back at her, as I sit in the armchair like a sullen teenager. My defiance is pathetic, like I'm a thirteen-year-old stomping her foot over going to the mall.

"If you don't want to talk, we can just sit here. I'm okay with the silence if you are." She tries again after a beat.

"You have to say that so you can bill my parents, or the army, or whoever the fuck is paying for this for a full rated hour," I bite back.

Dr. Liu chuckles. "Hey, nothing wrong with knowing my value and charging for it."

Hmm, not what I thought she'd say.

"Aren't you supposed to say that you're here to help me, no matter the cost? That financial gains mean nothing compared to my mental health, or some flowery shit like that?"

She tips her head, digesting my question. "That wouldn't be honest of me, would it? And I think you're a man who values honesty, Everett. Yes, my job puts me in a very well-off position financially. But I *do care* about the mental health of my patients. I wouldn't come here to sit in silence with the ones who have been through something very difficult if I didn't care."

How the hell did she know I value honesty? Is she a therapist, or a fucking mind reader?

We sit through most of the rest of the session in silence. Though after her comment about caring, I don't sulk quite as hard.

And when Dr. Liu says she's looking forward to seeing me next week, I don't protest or tell her I won't be there.

———

If it weren't for my best friend dragging me out of the house, I wouldn't leave it at all.

But Graden showed up shortly after my therapy session, ransacked my room, promised to pay for burritos, and basically did everything but give me a wedgie to get me up and out of bed. So here I am, dousing hot sauce on my free steak burrito and begrudgingly tolerating his conversation.

Graden has been my best friend since we were kids. The amount of time we've been called to the principal's office, served detention together, snuck out, partied too hard, won championship trophies ... together, we've done it all.

Well, almost everything. He opted for the college athlete route while I picked the military, so I guess he won the quality of life lottery on that deal. Somehow, fate knew he'd need to be home for this week, you know the week I came back from the dead. Although, I don't really believe in fate, so we'll blame the coincidence on his university's pre-planned fall break.

"So, can I see the tats?" Graden asks with a mouthful of spicy chorizo.

I squint a not-impressed expression at him. "No."

"Come on, dude. You bragged about all the ink you were sporting in those letters right before ..."

He breaks off, and I know what he was about to say. Right before I was captured. Right before I got gone. Right before I became missing in action.

What the people who silence themselves before they say that don't know is what that really means. Right before a bunch of fucking sand ghosts took hammers and drills to my body. Right before they starved me and kept me up for hours on end with rambling music or water torture. Right before they filmed four different videos in which I thought they'd saw my head off in another minute.

Shaking my head, I push the images into the dark box I've tried to secure them in at the back of my brain.

"Whatever, dude. You're not seeing them," I answer sternly.

Not only do I feel like an idiot for bragging about the full sleeves I had a military buddy ink my body with over there, but I don't want Graden to see the scars. To see the arm-length silvery patch where one of the enemy soldiers dragged a machete down my arm.

"Fine. Be that way. Hey, have you whined at your parents for the new Madden, yet? Bet you could ask for anything and they'd buy it."

He's always been good at distracting me from anything of a serious nature. Not that he wasn't a beast on the football field in high school; he wouldn't be the starting wide receiver at a division one college if he wasn't. But in terms of anything other than sports and training, you can count on Graden to be the quintessential class clown.

"Dude, Madden has been the last thing on my mind." But now that I think about it, video games might be a fun outlet, as long I don't have to shoot anything. "But bring it over tomorrow and I'll kick your ass."

"Oh, bro, don't even start. You haven't held a controller in a year, I'm going to wipe the fucking floor with you." He snorts, giving me a cocky grin.

This feels normal, the two of us shooting the shit. It almost makes me forget, for one second, how fucked up I am.

When Graden insisted on eating at Ocean Taco, the only Mexican joint in Brentwick, I hesitated. It's right on Dellan Drive, the main street in town, and anyone could see us. Or worse, we could run into a certain person I've been avoiding since I gave her verbal whiplash in my backyard.

But he told me to stop being a pussy, and no one had talked

back to me since I'd gotten home. It felt so good, that I relented and agreed to venture to the most public of streets in our hometown.

"Hey, man!" Graden rises halfway out of his chair, waving someone over.

When I turn, I notice Scott, a kid two years younger who played football with us back in high school, giving us the bro nod as he waits for change from the girl at the hostess stand.

Scott approaches us, the new captain of the football team from everything I've read in the local paper since I've been back. When you can't stand the white noise of a TV, too close to helicopter blades, and the frequency of the radio makes you jumpy, your last resort is old-fashioned reading.

"Hey, man! I didn't know you were home."

The two fist bump and do the half shoulder guy hug we're all universally versed in. Then he turns to me.

"Wow, Everett, great to see you, man." He holds out a fist, and I weakly bump it.

I'm having a problem with physical contact, no matter how much my brain rationally knows that these people aren't going to hurt me.

"Thanks. You too." Is it, though?

"What are you guys up to?" He eyes me cautiously, as if he's trying not to say the wrong thing or act like he hasn't just glimpsed someone who came back from the dead.

"Nothing, man. I'm home on fall break, just lying low with this guy. Had to come get some grub, it's too good to stay away. How about you, how is the season going?"

I tune them out as Scott regales Graden about the Brentwick football season, how they've won both games they've played, what the roster looks like. I focus on my burrito, cutting, forking, and chewing. Turning my hearing off is a new skill, one I'm glad to have mastered. Too much social interaction grates on my nerves these days.

"So you talked to Kennedy?" Scott says, and I'm slammed right back into the current moment.

I can tell he tried to bring it up organically, though his voice makes it sound anything but.

That's when I remember that he's dating Rachel, one of the girl next door's best friends.

I wonder if she's said something to her fucking cheerleading squad already. Probably whined about her crush snubbing her or some ridiculous shit that means nothing in the grand scheme of life. Why else would he be asking?

"Oh, man, she got hot since you've been away. Didn't you guys have some kind of fuck buddy pact if you ever came back?" Graden elbows me.

My gut roils, and I shoot him a look. "No, we didn't."

I don't bother answering the rest of his question, or responding to his speculation about her looks. We all know how much of a fucking knockout Kennedy is, it doesn't need to be said.

Scott looks back and forth between Graden and I, an awkward silence falling over us. "All right. Well, there is a barn party tonight if you guys want to come. I know it's just high school shit, but there will be kegs and weed."

He throws up a hand and departs as easily as he came.

Graden turns to me. "Let's go to that party."

"No." I immediately shut it down.

"Aw, come on, why not? Free beer, hot high school chicks, a little bit of fun. You remember fun, right?" His voice is a lesson in mocking.

"Fuck off. I just don't ... I don't want a crowd."

"Drink enough and you won't notice them. We're going."

Graden flips me off, and shoves a huge forkful of Mexican food mess into his mouth.

And because drinking a vat of alcohol to numb my brain actually does sound like a good idea, I don't argue.

Pulling my jacket more firmly around my shoulders, I snuggle into whatever warmth I can get.

"Can we please close the doors?" I whine again.

Judy, the head EMT at the Brentwick Rescue Squad, turns her kind blue eyes on me. "No can do, lady. If we get a call, you know the drill. Out the door as fast as we can."

A gust of wind blows through the two large garage doors at the front of the rescue squad building, past the two shining ambulances parked inside, and into my bones where I sit on a stool.

"I know, I know. It's just so cold!"

My EMT uniform is bulky and does insulate well, but it's an unseasonably cold September night, and I'm cranky. I knew I'd be working a late shift, but didn't realize it would be on the night that Rachel and Bianca wanted to throw the barn party. Now, I'd not only be late, but I'd be exhausted from however many emergency calls we'd make, and my hair would look like crap.

"You better get used to it. This winter is supposed to be brutal. Doesn't mean lives won't need saving in that frigid Jersey landscape." Judy tips her chin at me. "I did put a kettle on, so there will be warm tea soon enough."

Judy has been my boss here since I started about a year and a half ago. I took the EMT courses and got licensed shortly after turning sixteen, not only because it would look great for medical school, but because I am genuinely interested. Working a job that allows me to gain medical training, check out some pretty gnarly injuries, and pays? Yeah, sign me up.

Awaiting our tea, Judy sits on a stool next to me, listening to the scanner whistling and humming with different frequencies and talking on it. She's both motherly and stern, the perfect combination for this job. Judy is also a whiz when it comes to assessing a situation, triaging it, and getting the patient safely to a hospital in as little time as possible. She's been doing this for over twenty years, and I admire the crap out of her.

She's also got a sarcastic sense of humor, so she's my kind of people.

"Did you watch the new *Real Housewives of Beverly Hills*?" I ask, knowing she's just as much of a reality TV addict as I am.

"Yes! Can you believe that Erika spent thirty thousand dollars on a bag? What must it be like to have that kind of money?" she muses.

I chuckle. "You and I will *never* know."

"Don't sound so much like a bitter old maid, that's my job. But you're right." Judy grins and nods at me. "I just can't believe that new one pushed what's her name's dog in the pool."

"They totally need to recast her. She and her husband are *the* worst. If I have to hear that fake British accent one more time—"

I'm cut off by the whistling of the tea kettle, and about three seconds after that, a call comes in through the radio.

"Reporting a twenty-nine-D-one about a mile north of Dellan Drive. Code one, with a twenty-two-D-one. Four victims in total, a priority two, two priority threes and a thirty-B-two priority one. All units dispatch."

In seconds flat, Judy and I, plus the two other men on shift tonight, begin zipping up our uniforms, grabbing our go-bags, and loading into the ambulance. The call that came in is for an urgent, all sirens needed, major motor vehicle accident with victims trapped inside one or more vehicles. Two of the victims are not seriously injured, another is in serious condition, but possibly not life threatening, and the last victim has a serious hemorrhage and remains either unconscious, or was dead on arrival.

None of us talk to each other, the rhythm of our team a natural, practiced thing. We've all done this before, have worked in tandem, and know what needs to get put into that ambulance before we can go assess the damage. I grab my bag, a couple of IV bags that are meant to be refrigerated until use, a cooler full of blood bags, and then help James, one of the other EMTs, roll the traveling sonogram into the back of the vehicle. Having done my duties, I hop into the passenger seat and buckle up.

The adrenaline begins pumping through my chest, but I inhale slowly through my nose as Judy hops into the driver's seat beside me and cranks the lights and sirens on. Peeling out of the rescue squad building, we're on the road and headed to the crash scene.

No matter how many times I do this, there is always that initial moment of fear. I remember my first call, having Judy talk me through the gore and devastation I was about to see. She told me that as EMTs, we get one breath. One breath to inhale and exhale all the fear, nerves, doubts and jitters that would get in the way of our focus. Because once we're on the scene, dealing with people's lives, we don't get the luxury of hesitating. That advice has always stayed with me, and so I give myself one breath, and then plunge into the protocol of it all.

Judy's voice is forceful, direct. "I'll deal with the hemorrhage. James, I'll need you with me. Nicholas, you take the priority threes, and make sure they get blankets, water, just keep them calm and comfortable because this will be a long night with the police for them. Kennedy, you'll take the priority two."

Both James and Nicholas are older than me, have been doing this for longer. But Judy doesn't believe in that kind of structure, in giving us easy training. I've had a couple of patients code under my hands, I've plugged an artery, I've held the neck of a toddler stable while waiting for a back brace. The number of life altering procedures or moments of intense decision making I've experienced on this job have only made me stronger, and proven that this is what I want to do with my life.

We get to the scene in five minutes flat, the perks of being able to cut off anyone on the roads at this hour. From my vantage in the passenger seat. I can make out a car sitting on the side of the road with its flashers on, the guardrail next to it completely shredded to bits. I can't see the front, but I'll bet anything the entire hood is crunched in like a soda can.

"Keep your heads. Do your jobs," Judy instructs, and we all jump out, hauling medical supplies and our emergency bags.

The police are already there, and they fill us in using codes and shorthand speech. Two passengers sit on the ground near one of the three cop cars, and when Nicholas makes his way over to them, I know they're the priority threes. They wear shock and confusion on their faces, but neither looks injured beyond bumps and scrapes.

I can't tell what happened, how the crash occurred, but I know that my victim is somewhere down the ravine, trapped in the car. I'm going to have to get down there, but the police will have to consult me on how they're planning to make that happen. In this kind of situation, we want to get to the injured person as soon as possible, but it does no good to rush and risk injury to ourselves or someone else.

It's then that my eyes follow the direction everyone else seems to be looking.

A body lays haphazardly on the ground, probably thrown from the vehicle that went through the guardrail. The limbs are arranged in an unnatural fashion, broken in positions that couldn't possibly allow for a human being to be so quiet. Whoever this is, they lie face down on the dark gravel, and I can make out the pool of blood trickling from their abdomen.

Slowly, calmly, Judy walks toward her patient, the code one with a possible hemorrhage. She bends down, presses two fingers to the victim's neck, and then removes them.

"DOA," Judy announces, her expression one of practiced professionalism tinged with solemnness.

I blow out a breath, trying to tighten every muscle in my abdomen against the flood of nausea that sweeps through my stomach. There is one part of this job that will never become old hat, that my heart will never become accustomed to.

Seeing life leave another person's body, watching them die or bleed out, unable to save them … it steals a piece of my soul each time I watch it happen. I have no idea how Judy and my coworkers go back to normal life after this, as if it's just a job requirement to watch a human being expire.

Whenever I work a shift at the rescue squad, I know it will be a challenging, long night. But these are the kind that extinguish one of the finite rays of hope inside me.

EVERETT

J esus Christ, someone rewound my life and dropped me right back into high school.

At least, that's how I feel standing in the middle of the Johnstones field, next to their quintessential red barn, as hundreds of teenagers drink themselves stupid on shitty keg beer.

This was my stomping ground, back in the day, and I'm not surprised to see that it's lived on in our absence after we graduated. Kids were doing it before us, kids are doing it after us, and long after these drunk morons go off into the real world, some other teenagers will pick up the torch and run with it.

The Johnstones are one of the oldest families in Brentwick, the original nuclear family boasting nine children. The branches of the family down through the years have seen dozens of aunts, uncles, cousins, and grandkids take up residence in the town. I went to high school with approximately fifteen Johnstones, and I know there are more in the grades below me. The barn parties, like I said, started before I ever took my first sip of beer at fifteen, but they've always been located in the same place. The Johnstone's own many businesses, one being a fifty-acre farm on the outskirts of town. This barn has been abandoned since I don't know when, and it's common knowledge by both parents and cops that kids party here every Friday and Saturday night. The adults have always looked the other way.

Graden drags me out around eleven, well into the partying hour for these amateurs, all of whom probably have midnight curfews or are lying to their parents and claiming to be sleeping at a friend's house. So, when we arrive, the bonfire is roaring, the air stinks of marijuana, and a hundred or more drunk as fuck high school kids are making out, laughing their heads off, or singing to country music like they'll die tomorrow.

After grabbing two cups of mostly foam and a smidge of shit beer, I follow my best friend as he walks around fist bumping and dabbing people. A couple of the onlookers give me the once-over, and I know they know who I am. No one is going to broach the subject, or maybe someone drunk enough actually will.

"Let's get you laid tonight, brother. You need to let off some steam." Graden rubs his hands together, scoping out the party like a lion searching for the ripest kill.

"Let's not," I grumble, taking a swig of shitty keg beer.

I'd love to take a puff off the joint I smell so strongly in the air, but that would require chatting up a group and getting in on it, and I have no desire to talk to anyone else at this party.

"Come on, look at all of this available pussy. As long as they're eighteen, wrap it up and go to town." He pretends to smack a fake ass in front of his crotch.

"Smooth." I roll my eyes.

"You don't still have that card you took with you to Iraq, do you?" Graden eyes me curiously.

I turn my head, sipping my beer to avoid him.

"Holy fuck, you do. You've never gotten your dick wet, still to this day."

It's as if I've revealed that I'm really the son of an alien king, and I've come to take him back to the future with me. That's how much his eyes are bulging out of his head.

"Yell it fucking louder, why don't you?" I grumble, flipping him my middle finger.

It's pretty easy not to lose your fucking virginity when you're six feet deep in the ground being tortured on the regular. I won't say I wasn't tempted before that, when in high school and then there were options overseas. Female soldiers get just as lonely as male ones, and there were some locals who would come around. When I still attended school in Brentwick, it's not as if the invitations weren't plentiful; I was the quarterback of the football team for fuck's sake. If I'd wanted to screw someone, I could have by now.

But what I never told Kennedy was that, while she was holding out for her first kiss, I was waiting to ... lose it to her. That sounds fucking corny now, like I was some poetic sap who believed in romance and everlasting love. I guess at that point I kind of did. But now, it feels so fucking stupid.

I'm a twenty-year-old who has shot and killed people, but never got my nut off in a chick.

"How the hell is this even possible? That's it, now we're really finding you a fuck buddy for the night." The hard set of my friend's jaw tells me that he's actually going to put this plan in motion.

A gust of wind blows past me, taking the heat of the fire on its tail, and that's when I hear her laugh.

I should have known she'd be here. Hell, she came flouncing out of her car the first day I got back to Brentwick in her cheer-leading uniform. And if there is anything I know about these parties, it's that cheerleaders and jocks always attend. I should know, I was in that crowd.

Kennedy stands across the field, the bonfire between us, so every time it moves as I try to get a good look at her, it appears as if tiny sparks of light are glittering off her skin. It might be a cold autumn night, but by the way she's cracking a smile and shaking her hips to the latest Luke Combs song, you'd think the long-sleeve painted to her curves and the jeans plastered to her long, slim legs were made of fleece.

All those dark brown curls swirl around her face as she chats with her friends or slings her arms around a different guy's shoulder every other minute. The energy coming off of her is electric, there is no way I can keep my eyes off of her.

She's wearing a sweater that shouldn't even be legal. It's tight as hell, the round globes of her curvy tits pressing against the pink fluff. The V splitting the neck wide open reveals her ample cleavage, and instantly, I'm sporting a semi.

Fuck me. Apparently, since returning home, I've forgotten my dick. Some quality jack off time is in order to keep the horny guy under control.

Because, as unbelievable as Kennedy looks, sipping from a red solo cup across the bonfire, she is off-limits. Not only did she fucking break the promise she made to me, but falling down that rabbit hole will only destroy us both. I'm not the guy she used to moon over, and I'd be a complete idiot not to know she used to harbor a cruise-sized crush for me. Maybe she still does, why else would she bring up the kiss?

A flashback in my mind lands me in this very field, Kennedy on my lap, my fingers playing dangerously with the hem of her thin camisole. Fuck, how many times had I almost brought her back into those woods and undressed her perfect little body? We used to flirt toward the edge of a cliff during these parties, but I'd always held myself back.

Spoiler alert, I used to harbor an Everest-sized crush on her, too.

But I'm a different person now. The kind of man that dashes her hope and slut shames her. The man who can only tell her about vivid nightmares, not take part in the dreams of her future. The soldier who turned against his country.

No one can learn my secret, least of all Kennedy. What would she think of me? How would she respond, knowing I landed myself in that godforsaken torture camp trying to protect the people I was supposed to fight against?

I turn away, actively trying not to have her in my line of sight. If one of these fuckboys starts groping on her, I'm not sure I can be counted on to control my temper. As much as I tell myself I want no part of her, if I see her with her tongue down another guy's throat, I'll probably cut his right out.

It's maybe a minute before I hear a commotion coming from the direction I just purposely turned away from, and I can't help myself. I turn to watch.

Kennedy, her two best friends, Rachel and Bianca, and a couple of other girls I don't recognize, stand in a circle, raising shot glasses into the air. They chant some line about being friends forever, and then toss them back, a lot of the party-goers cheering wildly after the girls come up, sputtering for beer or something to chase with.

The rest of the girls calm down, either meandering off or falling into each other's arms to dance. But Kennedy lingers by the guy with the bottle.

"Give me another!" she demands, accepting a shot glass full of liquid less than thirty seconds after she took the first one.

Although, who knows if that's her first one. Kennedy looks like she might not be able to stand on her own, she's swaying so much. She knocks back the second shot, that I'm aware of, and screws up her face in a sour reaction. Immediately, she chugs beer out of her red cup to wash the burn of alcohol down.

"And another!" Her lithe body wiggles, shaking the ass I can't make out past the flames and logs between us.

I watch as Rachel and Bianca's eyes widen, but they don't stop her. Maybe they think it's funny she's trying to lose all control. Maybe they don't think they can stop her.

"I think that's enough."

I don't even realize I've walked halfway across the field, right up into Kennedy's personal space, until I'm pulling the shot out of her readily waiting grasp.

"Hey, man, what the—" The guy who was serving from a magnum bottle of Svedka is about to start yapping at me, until he sees my face.

His "oh, shit" expression is all I need to see to know that he knows who I am.

"What the hell!" Kennedy makes a face at him, before turning to me.

Her expression molds from annoyance into shock in one second flat. Then, she smacks me with an open palm, right against my right pec.

"Everett? What the hell do you think you're doing? That's mine!" Her words are clear, but the screech of her frustrated tone grates on my ears.

"Doesn't look like it anymore." In one quick swallow, I down the shot.

The liquor burns my throat, dissolving the knot of fury that took up residence there just seconds ago as I watched Kennedy making one bad decision after the next.

"You're cut off. She's cut off, got me?" I say to those around us, who nod like bobble heads.

They're probably scared shitless of me, which means ridiculous rumors about my time away have been floating around. That's probably better, they should be.

"You're not the boss of me!" Kennedy shrieks, rage flashing in those amber eyes.

It turns me on, her anger, and the tip of my cock is tingling with anticipation. *Fuck, keep it together, Everett.* How did I go from actively trying to avoid her, to stomping across the party and rubbing my scent all over her? I told her I wanted nothing to do with her.

"And you sound like a five-year-old," I taunt.

She stamps her foot, really adding to the level of maturity. "What are you even doing here? This is for Brentwick seniors only."

"Yet I see Dan and Matt Gilroy over there, both juniors." I hold up a hand, waving to the twin little brothers of one of my good friends from school.

Kennedy huffs out an annoyed breath. "Either way, you have no say in what I do and don't do. You made it very clear the other day that you never wanted one."

People around us are starting to stare, and both Rachel and Bianca, who stand close by, look stunned. This is not a conversation I want to have, much less in front of people, and yet I'm the one who came swooping in like some sober savior.

Attempting to reclaim her shot glass, Kennedy swats at my hand, getting into my space so much that I have to wrap a hand around her waist to keep her upright as she clumsily paws at me.

"Let. Me. Have. It," she grits out, struggling to even move with the hold I have on her.

Somehow, she's able to slip from my grip, and sidles back up to Bottle Guy, taking the entire handle of Svedka and gulping.

"What the fuck ..." My teeth snap together, and I grab it, spilling vodka all over the ground.

"That's it," I declare, and pluck her straight off her feet.

With Kennedy over my shoulder, and a handle of vodka in my fist, I take a swig, hand it back to the random guy, and stomp off.

"You are a piece of shit!" she curses, smacking my ass and digging her nails into my tailbone.

It's the first I've heard her curse ... maybe *ever*. It turns me on more than anything. Well, that and the fact that she's swatting at my ass. Any kind of female contact at this point would probably turn me on.

"Yeah, I know. Welcome to reality," I grumble, because I am a piece of shit.

But I'm a piece of shit who isn't going to let her get alcohol poisoning out in this fucking field. Who isn't going to let some drunk asshole take advantage of her unconscious body. I'm going to put a stop to that *right now*.

Setting her down after walking into a clearing, the laughter and music long behind us, I watch as Kennedy rights her clothes and huffs like a pissed off peacock. It's hard to take her frustration seriously when her tits are covered in bubble gum pink fuzz.

"So I'm not allowed to lay a finger on you, but you can throw me over your shoulder like some kind of Neanderthal?" She sways, disoriented from the vodka and her little upside-down ride.

"What the hell were you doing back there, Kennedy?" I demand.

"You're not the only one who sees dead people." Her voice takes on a singsong quality.

"What is this, comparing our *Sixth Sense* abilities?" I crack, the vodka going to my head. It's been a minute since I've drank, and the liquor is pulling me into the realm of tipsy.

Kennedy cracks up, leaning on me for support. The side of her boob brushes my bicep, and the jolt goes straight to my balls. If I'm not careful, and she keeps touching me, I won't be able to keep myself in check. As it is, the hormones raging through me were sent into chaos the minute I took her out here in the dark, alone.

And as much as I told her that touching me was a hard limit now, no alarm bells go off in my head. I don't want to put her in a headlock or cower in a corner when her hand grips my arm, and I'm ... fucking shocked.

"Remember when we secretly watched that movie as kids, and then I had night terrors for like, weeks? My mom was convinced I was having a psychotic break."

"Yeah, then I came clean and got grounded for being a bad influence on you."

In fact, I often got grounded for being a bad influence on Kennedy. She was my only playmate, both of us being only children, and it was only natural that the boy took the brunt of the punishment.

The cold closes in, as does the darkness, and no one is coming out here after us. I miscalculated just how tense removing her from that situation would be, because it landed me in my own personal hell.

Kennedy shivers, moving in closer, and though I shouldn't be able to stand so close to someone due to all I've been put through, I don't step back. If anything, I lean in.

We're pushed up against each other, her tits against my chest, my groin snug against her hips. All of the blood in my body rushes to my cock, and she must notice the massive hard-on I'm beginning to sport. Our breath comes out in white puffs, the air and the proximity to her making it hard to breathe for me.

"What do you mean, you see dead bodies?" Something about her is off tonight, and I can't put my finger on it.

And it's spooky that even after all the time I've been away, I can still read and know her moods like the back of my hand.

Kennedy ignores my question. "I miss those days," she whispers, those doe eyes blinking up at me.

The moon illuminates her face, and all the reasons why I shouldn't kiss her no longer remain in my brain. I promised her this; we promised each other this. We could still have it ...

A shriek pierces the night air, some girl out in the woods, probably with a guy chasing her as foreplay. It breaks the spell.

"Yeah, well, I'm not the same person I was. We're not the same."

I physically remove her hands from my arms and step back, severing the connection. I take two more steps back, trying to convey to Kennedy that she should go. That I don't want any part of this. She gets the message, turning without a word to walk off.

Just when I think she's going to rejoin her friends, Kennedy stops, her back to me. When she speaks, her voice seems a million miles away. "Yeah, I guess we're not."

Two days after the barn party, after the Monday-est Monday anyone has ever lived through, I flop down on my bed with my trigonometry and physics text-books, not eager to dive in.

Why does there still have to be so much homework, especially when it's senior year? Oh, right, when my dumb ass decided to take advanced placement courses during the coasting period for most of my other classmates.

I figure, though, that if I can place out of most math courses in college, that would be better for my grade point average. Science is my easiest subject, obviously, and I can pick up English and history well enough. But it's math that gives me a run for my money. Not that I don't still ace tests and walk out with one of the highest grades for the marking period, but it takes me triple the amount of time to study for those tests or complete that homework than it does anything else. I know that college-level math will only be increasingly harder, which is why I'm busting my butt to place out of the requirement before I get there.

A knock comes at my closed bedroom door, and I yell that

it's open. My mom walks in, two glasses of iced tea in her hands, and a tray of cookies teetering on one arm.

"Oh! How did you know I needed study snacks?" I push up on my elbows from my stomach, where I was about to flip open the trig assignment.

Mom raises her eyebrow. "Because I birthed you and I know everything you need, every second."

"Well, that's kind of a creepy answer. But, I'll take it since you brought cookies. Sugar?" My fingers are crossed when I hold them up.

"With funfetti frosting, your favorite. How you don't have a million cavities is beyond me." She chuckles.

Sweets during studying is my weakness, and I'm studying a lot due to my classes so there are a lot of sweets.

Mom sets them down, hands me one, and then takes a sip from her glass. When she spots two sets of pom-poms laying across my floor, she rolls her eyes and starts laughing.

"You did not snatch Bianca's pom-poms again."

"You bet I did." I hold my chin high with pride. "Technically, it's not stealing if your forgetful best friend leaves them on the second set of bleachers in the gym. It's my captain-ly duty to collect them. And then maybe leave them on top of the flagpole, or on the bookshelf in Mr. Greyman's office."

It's a running prank between Rachel, Bianca, and I. Bianca is constantly misplacing things, most of all her cheerleading para-phernalia. Last year, Rachel stapled Bi's pom-poms to a bulletin board in our French teacher's classroom, I hung them from a fluorescent light in the cafeteria—which took almost breaking my neck after Scott hoisted me on his shoulders while standing on a lunchroom table—and the rest of the team helped us tie one pom-pom around a brick and sink it to the bottom of the gymnasium pool.

"What's your plan for them this time?" Sitting on my bed,

her fingers skim the pages of my textbooks, noting what subjects I'm about to binge learn.

I shrug. "No clue. Rachel is supposed to have some devious plan, so I'll follow her lead."

"You stay at Rachel's on Saturday night?" she asks out of nowhere.

My parents are epically cool. Especially since I'm an only child. Most people would assume they smother me, that we're too close, or that I'm a spoiled brat. In reality, they give me a long leash, trust me to make smart choices, reward me for the good grades and community work I do, and show me unconditional love while keeping open communication. A lot of people out there think being an only child holds negative connotations, but I choose to focus on the positives.

However, this is the part where I feel epically guilty. Because I didn't stay at Rachel's, though I told them I would and even texted that we were back at her parent's place. In reality, our group of seniors passed out under the stars at the barn party, covered in layers of fleece blankets by the fire. We could have died from burns, hypothermia, or a random serial killer hacking us all to death, but we survived—not without brutal hangovers in the morning though.

"Yep, we went to the diner in the morning." I smile, trying my best to sound nonchalant and genuine.

If Mom suspects that I'm lying, she doesn't say anything. This is also a good aspect to our relationship; she doesn't snoop or push for answers. My parents putting their faith in me to make the right choices, and giving me space to do so, usually means I *do* make the smart decision. Just not every single time. Saturday night was an exception. I had way too much to drink to numb the shock of what I'd seen at the accident. When there are dead bodies floating around in your memory, you don't feel like remembering much of the night.

"All right, sweetheart. Well, have fun with your homework. I'll come up and check on you in another hour or so." She lays a kiss on my forehead and walks out.

Staying true to her word, Mom does come and check on me in an hour. I've gotten through all of my trig assignment, most of the history paper I already have due in the first month of school, and am on to my physics homework when she comes up. Blinking and rubbing the study haze out of my eyes, I decide to call it a night.

But my laptop seems to shine from my desk like a beacon out of a corny eighties movie, special effects and all, because I've been ignoring it. It's almost the last week of September, every one of my college applications is filled out and ready to go, and I know which programs are at the top of my list. But I can't send any of them.

Because I haven't been able to write more than five words of an essay without deleting it.

Chastising myself, because I'm anything if not punctual and a go-getter, I march over to my desk and flip my computer open. Damn this writer's block, damn this essay, I'm going to make it my bitch.

As my fingers ghost over the keys, not selecting any letters but merely going through the motions of typing, I know what I should write about. I know the one thing that will sincerely come from within me, but I'm freaking terrified of opening that Pandora's box.

My mind flashes back to the body on the pavement during my last EMT shift, and how unnatural it was to just pack up and leave after all our other work had been completed. How empty I felt, how absolutely devastating witnessing that loss of life was.

And the age-old question I've been asking myself since I decided on my dream comes rushing back: How am I supposed to be an effective nurse, how can I care for some of the most critical patients, when I fear them dying?

Death, loss, tragic or otherwise, it's a part of the profession. You see it nearly every day when you work in a hospital, and I've seen it more than once as an EMT. My coworkers, Judy, and most if not all of the nurses and doctors I've worked with on transfers when I ride up to the hospital in an ambulance are so accustomed to death, it doesn't much faze them anymore.

But I, for some reason, just can't get past it. How do I give my all to a profession, to saving the lives of others, when I know that in a lot of the cases, the outcome won't be positive?

Why can't I admit that this unnerves me so much? I think because if I do, I'll be admitting that I'm not fit to be a nurse. I'm not fit to be in a field where we are forced to cut a piece of our souls out to give the medical care someone might need, even if it doesn't necessarily save their life.

I stare at the blinking cursor of my Word document for far longer than I anticipated to, until the clock reads an hour or so later that all I can do is stumble into bed, defeated by the essay once again.

I n the end, Rachel and I affix Bi's pom-poms to the school banner hanging over the glass-walled office of the principal.

Technically, Rachel does it because no way in hell was I sneaking into the school at six a.m. to pull that prank. But it had its desired effect, the round of applause by those students who know about the ongoing joke. The school week, aside from the prank, has gone on uneventfully. The three of us, and their boyfriends, eat breakfast at our usual table in the cafeteria, text secretly in classes, gossip during gym, and just do general high school kid stuff.

I meet them at Angelo's, the local pizza place, to do homework. Which really means Bianca fills us in on her boyfriend spelling the alphabet in her ... um, private places. Apparently, this is a thing. Not that my inexperienced ass would know. I feel like such a fool now, having waited all this time for Everett. Not that I would have been letting a guy draw the ABCs with his tongue, I'm definitely not ready for that, but I could have been dating. I could have been kissing. I could have trained my mind not to think about the boy next door.

Even though I try with all my might, I still look at the closed curtains of his windows in the shadows of my room. I haven't seen him since he threw me over his shoulder that night of the barn party and nearly kissed me in the woods. I thought he was going to fulfill his promise right there, and I wasn't drunk enough to forget the way our bodies touched.

But, my life doesn't revolve around that any longer. It can't. So, I go about my regularly planned life. And that means that at the end of every day, we attend cheer practice.

Rach lies on the bleachers after practice ends, a lollipop in her mouth, while Bi takes out a bottle of nail polish and sets to painting her fingers candy apple red. I just shake my head, directing my attention back to the binder of choreography I've been mulling over before our season even started. We have about a month before our first cheer competition, and we're slowly but surely putting together a kick-ass routine.

As much as our high school, and the parents of the football players who come to the games, thinks that the cheerleading squad is just a bunch of skinny girls wearing a lot of makeup and shaking their chests—we're not. Our practices are focused, our strength and endurance can measure up to the best wide receivers on the football team, and we put together a mean tumbling and stunt routine to compete against the top high schools in the state. Last year, we were runner-up at the state cheerleading competition, and stamped our tickets to the nationwide competition in Disney World.

It's my job as captain to formulate a difficult and show-stopping routine, combining tumbling, a prideful cheer, and death-defying stunts. The music has to be perfect, it has to pump up the crowd and make them think what we're doing is easy, when it's totally not.

Though the last of the warm days are upon us, and the sun is setting earlier than it did during the hot summer break, the sky is turning a burnt orange and the breeze is comfortable. It's just the three of us, not wanting to drive home yet, riding out the last year of high school as long as we can.

"So, can we discuss the elephant sitting on the town of Brentwick?" Rachel yawns, stretching out until her shirt rides up over her impressive abs.

"I wasn't aware there was a zoo animal sitting on the town." I chuckle, making a swipe across my page with a red pen.

Bi shoots me a look. "She's talking about you and Everett. Or are we just going to keep on pretending that the soldier next door who promised to kiss you hasn't returned home and then dragged you into the woods at the barn party?"

I'm so damn shocked that my typically flighty, unconcerned friend just smacked me with a two-by-four of honesty. Seriously, I drop my pen and stare at her, my jaw nearly on the turf I'm sitting on.

Rachel pushes up suddenly, her elbows resting on her knees. "Yeah, I can't do this anymore. We've been keeping our distance on the subject for what feels like a fucking eternity, and I'm done. Did he fuck you against a tree? Did you whisper sweet nothings? Did the war turn him into a beast, all that pent-up sexual tension unleashing on you? God, tell me it was the last one. Make my dreams come true."

Honestly, I'm so stunned, I can barely roll my eyes at Rachel's ridiculous fantasies.

Bianca nods emphatically. "Please tell us you guys have snuck out and like done it in one of your backyards or something!"

"You think that if I lost my virginity, I wouldn't call both of you immediately after?" I give her a knowing look, and they shrug their shoulders.

"You know, I thought you'd be freaking out way more than you have since he came home," Bianca points out.

"I am freaking out." I sigh and realize I've been waiting to get this burden off my chest. "I just ... I don't know how to talk about it. I feel like I've spent years gushing to you guys about 'when Everett comes home' or this fairy tale that's always been in my brain."

"And we've been wholeheartedly beside you. I mean, some of the things he wrote you, the way he used to look at you, hold you ... it's obvious there is some off the charts chemistry there." Rachel gives me a thumbs-up.

Bianca flutters her eyelashes. "Right? And the serendipity of it all, it was just too good not to root for."

"Did you just say serendipity? Jesus, you guys are both freaking me out even more." I shake my arms, as if I have the heebie-jeebies.

"We've been waiting eons for this info. Neither one of us wanted to come on strong, because you tend to shell up. Especially when it comes to Everett. Come on, give us the details. How do you feel? You've obviously seen each other." Rachel gives me the knowing look only your best friend can give.

Closing my binder, I send a thanks up to the universe for giving me the two very best friends a girl could ever ask for. They know me, enough to lay off the Everett gossip until he'd been back for a while and I could get my head around it. Not that my head is anywhere near *around* what he'd said to me or how harsh he'd been, but at least I had time to process by myself.

"I talked to him the first week of school. He was in the backyard when I got home after practice, and I just walked up to him. You both know I saw him when the military brought him home, and he just looked so ... spooky. Like he was haunted, from the inside out. From the minute I laid eyes on him, I just ... I can't even describe it. All of those things we said and wrote to each other, they all came rushing back. So when I saw him, I hugged him. It was so stupid of me. Anyways, he shoved me off, yelled at me. Told me he was dead, got so pissed off when he found out I kissed someone else—"

"Wait a minute, how did that come up?" Bianca screeches, moving to sit right beside me.

I shrug. "He asked me."

"Oh, he brought that shit up? Boy is still in deep if he went through war and lived through torture and the first thing he wants to know is if you kept your kiss virginity." Rachel rubs her hands together.

But my hair just shakes in my face as I signal no. "I think he was just trying to shove my life in my face. He's so angry. Furious, at the world. Which, I guess he has a right to be. He basically told me he had no interest in ever speaking to me again, and then he showed up to the barn party."

"I could kill Scott, by the way. He invited him, I had no idea he was coming. If I did, I would have totally cooked up a plan to get you that kiss that night." Rachel rolls her eyes.

"It wouldn't have made a difference. Plus, I was drunk out of my mind. The EMT shift really messed me up. It was unexpected that he got all protective about me doing shots. I don't even know why he cared, he basically tore me down verbally in every way in his backyard.

"Because the boy is in love with you. Always has been." Rach gives me a *duh* expression, and swirls the lollipop around in her mouth.

"He's been through a very difficult thing," Bianca says solemnly. "But, I agree with Rach. He asked about the kiss. He came to the barn party knowing you'd be there. And that whole chivalrous, throw-you-over-his-shoulder? Shit, that was hot. You could feel the lust rolling off him. No matter what you've both been through, the fuck-me eyes are still there between you."

Just thinking about Everett pressing up against me in the woods has my heart shuddering, trying to catch its beat.

"Whenever I envisioned the boy I'd … you know." An angry blush marks my cheeks.

"The boy you'd have sex with. It's not a taboo subject, Kenny. Everyone in the world has sex, in some form or another. There are people out there who are kinky as fuck, who like to use whips and chains—"

I cut Rachel off. "That's more than enough, thanks. I don't know, I'm just not as open about this as you guys. I've always envisioned my first time, my first love, this sounds so stupid, but I imagined it would be with Everett. Now, I kind of feel like the idiot who planned her wedding when she was five and it will never work out the way she thought it would. He is so beyond damaged, and I have to adjust my mind to that. He's not the Everett we knew, the last name I scribbled in my notebooks. That much he's told me. I need to kick this school girl crush and get on with my life."

Rachel eyes me like a hawk. "And that's really what you want to do? Be over him?"

As much as my heart is screaming no at me, I know it's the only choice I have.

"Yes." I try to make my nod as decisive as possible, so she knows I'm serious.

Bianca's expression is resolved, and she blows on her nails. "All right then. We're going to have you out there dating so much, you're not going to have a free night of the week!"

I roll my eyes. "Let's please not call it dating. We're in high school, the most we do is show up to a party, make out with a guy, and hope he wants to hold our hand in the hallway in the days following."

Rachel snickers. "Or in Bi's case, have sex in the second-floor bathroom by Miss Howe's science classroom."

Bianca sticks her tongue out. "You're just mad Scott isn't into public displays of affection."

We all remember the screaming match they got into when Scott asked Rachel not to sit on his lap during lunch junior year. It was like an atomic bomb could have been dropped at any moment.

"True, I'm a little butthurt about it still. But he's so freaking hot, I don't care. I get him in private, which can be enough for me. But yes, we're going to set it up so that the hottest guy in school is your next crush. He can even be a friend-with-benefits if you don't feel like a boyfriend."

"Do I strike you as the friend-with-benefits type, Rach?" I chuckle, because she's known me long enough to know that's not the route for me.

"Well, no. But, you can be into a guy without picturing your wedding or making vows of undying love while listening to Taylor Swift in your bedroom." She stares pointedly.

I don't do that. Well, maybe I haven't done that. In, like, a month or so. Whatever.

As we pack up our things and then walk to our respective cars, my air blown kiss a goodbye as I duck into my driver's seat, I can't help but feel bittersweet. I'm glad my friends got me to open up about Everett, but it feels like talking about the brutal way he spoke to me and how he's not the same boy, well, it feels like an ending. It feels like an acknowledgment that all the things I wanted to come true, never will.

But at the same time, maybe this is the push I needed. To put myself out there, to consider other guys.

My heart aches with the thought that I'll never know how it truly feels to call Everett Brock mine, but it flutters thinking about the attention that might be heading its way.

11

EVERETT

"Are you glad to be home?"

Dr. Liu poses this question in our third therapy session as if it has an easy answer. I could tell her yes or no, but I know that's not what she's looking for. She'll just give me that stern stare that we both know I know better.

"That's not an easy question to answer." I give it to her straight.

Last session, I answered more than two questions she asked, though begrudgingly. They didn't scratch the surface, were just one-offs with no real thinking to be done on my part, but I think she counts it as a victory. I'm actually speaking to her, which I guess is her whole point to this.

"How so?" she pushes me, nodding her head as if to tell me to go on.

I sigh, raking a hand through my hair. "What you're asking essentially boils down to if I'm happy to be back in Brentwick, rather than living in a filthy pit having my organs rearranged each day. Would I rather be out in the fucking middle of nowhere, gunning people down? Or sitting on my bed, in my hometown, fucked up from PTSD? There really isn't a preferable answer, but any sane person would choose Brentwick. Though you and I know I'm suffering just as much as I was there."

"Thank you for sharing that with me." Her pen scribbles across her notebook. "Was the military your first choice?" She changes directions, and I didn't think she'd go this way.

I shrug. "If you mean, did I think about doing anything else after high school, then no."

"Why is that? You seem like a bright young man, I'm sure you could have gone to college. You played a sport, yes?"

I nod. "Football."

"Did you ever think about pursuing it after high school?" she asks.

Sure, I had. I don't know why, but it never appealed to me on a collegiate or professional level. The reason I loved playing football was because I got to do so with my best friends. With the coaches who had been with us since pee-wee days. I got to fuck around in the locker room, wear a varsity jacket, and walk out to a song I picked under those Friday night lights. There is a completely different atmosphere around high school football as opposed to the higher levels of the sport. I was passionate about the team game, not besting other athletes. So, I never really considered trying to go pro.

"No. I didn't."

"But you liked the sport when you played in high school?"

"What are you trying to get at?" I practically sneer because I don't need anyone to try to prod me in any direction.

Dr. Liu levels me with a gaze. "You don't want to address what happened when you were imprisoned. And you're telling me that you're not happy at home, that you can't move past what happened. The next best thing we can do is try to manually help you move on. I want you to think about what you liked before going into the military. It could be the simplest of things. Football in high school. A certain book. A slice of pizza you craved at the local Italian restaurant. Where are the things you found joy? Pick one and pursue it as a hobby or a job. Did you like working with your sports team? Go volunteer as a coach. You need to occupy your mind and your hands, because the last thing you should be doing is sitting inside, stewing. If you're not ready to talk, then involve yourself in the community so at least you can begin to go back to a civilian life."

"That sounds stupid as fuck." Deflection is a great way to not do what's being asked of you.

A stern brow gets thrown my way. "Do the homework. Or next session, I'm going to ask you to open up about the day you were captured."

Is it me, or is Dr. Liu busting my chops? She seems half-serious, and thinking about the day my tank exploded and I was carted off by screaming terrorists makes me want to black out and go catatonic.

So, instead, I'll think about the pizza I was passionate about and figure out a way to fulfill her ask. Because there is no way in hell I'm ever discussing that day in the desert.

I'm sitting out on the patio in my backyard, hours later, when my dad walks out.

"Oh, Ev, I didn't, uh, didn't see you there." He's jumpy, as he has been since the second I returned home.

"Yeah," I answer, though he didn't ask a question and my response hasn't furthered the conversation.

I've been sitting here thinking about what I could possibly do to satisfy Dr. Liu's request. I could get a menial job, sling pizzas or drive a fucking Uber. That is, if my parents ever give me driving privileges back. Not that I've even asked, but they've kept me bubble wrapped and I can pin blame on anyone these days without having to point a finger at myself.

There is also the possibility of college, since my military benefits would pay for it. But am I really going to sit in a classroom again? I hated learning through high school, why would I want to do it now?

"You had therapy today?" He nods, in a way that indicates he's trying to start conversation with me but doesn't know how.

Dad was my little league coach, the one who taught me how to throw a spiral. We went on camping trips; he taught me how to drive, bought me my first box of condoms which no, I haven't used but he probably thinks I have. My point is, he and I were as close as a father and son could be, especially since I was his only child. And now he has no idea how to treat me.

That's fair, I guess because I have no idea how to treat me. Or my parents, for that matter.

"Yes. You saw Mom drive me there." My voice conveys the *duh* unmistakably.

Dad nods again, and I really wish he'd stop doing that. "Are you hungry? We could go get sandwiches from The Delicious Delight."

The place used to be my favorite; we'd split a turkey sub and an Italian sub, with extra sour and cream and onion chips on the side.

"Not hungry." I don't even look at him.

I don't know why I'm being such an asshole. Maybe it's Dr. Liu in my head, taunting me for not knowing that next direction my life will go in.

"I don't know what to say to you, Everett." His voice is reed thin and desperate.

"Don't worry, Dad, no one does," I assure him in a cynical way.

Hanging his head, a defeated man, my father doesn't lash

out with an angry barb. I wonder, idly, if he and Mom have done coping therapy of their own. Maybe even before I got home.

When he begins to walk off, dejected, a twinge of guilt flicks me in the heart.

"Dad?"

He halts his progress, turning to look at me. There is so much hope in his eyes, and I want to tell him that he's not the type of man I've turned into. He hasn't seen the things I have; he hasn't felt real pain. The loss of his child, when he thought I was dead, is nothing in comparison to the raw, unfiltered agony I've felt to the core of my bones.

But I can't say that. The brand of honesty I brought back from war with me would slay people, completely gut them until they can't even breathe.

"Yes?" Dad waits patiently.

"I think I'm going to ask Coach Rott if I can help out with the football team at the high school."

It's an olive branch, one I'm extending because some tiny shred of my dilapidated heart feels fucking awful for all I've put my parents through.

His face lights up, every wrinkle I've caused on his face creasing. "I think that's a wonderful idea."

12

KENNEDY

The entire football stadium is abuzz with activity immediately after the last bell of the day.

My cheerleaders are busy on one side of the turf, stretching and pulling on their sneakers, adjusting hair into ponytails, sneakily flirting with the other athletes jogging around the track.

The football team comes out of the locker room in their pads just as the track team starts their laps, and the field hockey girls are over on the far end practicing shooting drills into a goal. It's high school personified, you can practically smell the teen spirit.

I join my friends, working my way from bicep stretches across my chest to dropping down into all three splits, my muscles fighting me each way. I haven't been as diligent this season with keeping up my stretches or strength conditioning. As one of the three flyers on the team, it's imperative that my body be strong and capable. But with college looming around the corner, and the admissions process sapping my energy, it's hard to focus on anything else.

"Oh my God, what is he doing here?"

At the shocked words of my best tumbler, Maya, half the

team turns their heads. I'm slow on the uptake, focusing on getting our routine music cued up on my phone and connected to the Bluetooth speaker I brought.

So it isn't until a few minutes after everyone else that my sights land on Everett Brock, standing on the sideline with a Brentwick hat covering his sandy blond hair and a whistle dangling from those full, red lips.

"What is he doing here?" I hiss to Rachel, who is close enough to me that no one else hears.

"I have no clue," she mutters. "He might be watching practice?"

That one's loud enough for the other squad members to hear, and one of our fliers, Georgia, volunteers an answer. "My dad is like, b-f-f's with Coach Rott, and he said that Everett Brock is going to be an assistant coach this season."

Panic fills my chest cavity, and I think my stomach just dropped into the balls of my feet.

Bianca rushes over, not so subtly, and presses a hand to my arm. "You okay?"

It takes me a minute to collect myself, but I steel my spine and tip my chin up. "Yeah, let's warm up."

Rachel eyes me for another second, and I give a slight shake of my head, warning her off. I promised myself, and them, that I was done with this school girl crush. But the urge to turn and stare at him, when he's this close, is so difficult to stave off.

"Just focus on Logan." Bianca wiggles her eyebrows.

Since I told them I'd be open to talking to other guys a couple of days ago, my two besties have been hard at work selecting the perfect candidate. Logan Myers is a senior on the football team, tall with the perfect athlete's body and a head full of dark curls. He's supposedly pretty nice, and though we haven't been in the same classes, he's smart enough to be in the same AP level as I am.

And apparently, Rachel has already found out he's interested in me, if I'm game.

Turning to look at him, I do have to admire how well he fills out the practice uniform. A moment later, as if he feels me staring at him, he turns and smiles, offering up a little wave. I smile shyly.

"Myers! Get back to work. What do you think this is, fucking Daydream Land?" Everett barks at the top of his lungs.

I can feel the ire of his tone all the way across the field, and when my mouth falls open slightly, he returns my shocked gaze with a stony grimace.

"Well, if he wasn't trying to pee all over his territory ..." Rachel snorts.

"Yeah, Kenny, I don't think you need to worry whether he likes you or not." Bianca pats me on the shoulder.

Shaking my head, because I need to lead my team right now, I instruct my squad to stretch, and start working on their tumbling skills for the first half of practice.

As the afternoon sun twinkles into early dusk, it's hard not to feel his presence. To feel my skin prickle every time my vision turns his way. There is an electric current running across the stadium, connecting the two of us like poles on opposite ends of the earth. I wonder if Everett feels this, too.

From tumbling, we move into cheer work, and then stunt work. One of the girls almost falls out of her liberty pose, and we can't seem to get our basket tosses right today. But we are getting stronger in terms of having four girls on the team who can do full twisting back flips, so there is a plus.

Before I know it, practice is over, and most of the athletes are heading to the locker room to shower and change. Here's the thing about being a cheerleader, we don't get a designated locker room space. I, and a rotation of the other girls on the squad, have to unload and load a tiny closet designated for our things before and after every practice.

I'm sweating and panting by the time I make it back out to the turf to collect my things and finally head home.

"Kennedy." His shadow falls over me as I hurry to collect my things.

I haven't spoken to him since the night of the barn party. He hasn't apologized, hasn't even bothered to peek out of his curtains, and hasn't shown up in town anywhere. And even though I told Rachel and Bianca I was done being hung up on my Everett fantasies, it's hard to stick to that resolve when he's standing in front of me, on my turf. Technically, I guess this was his turf first. And he doesn't even know that I'm peeved, well, not that I've explicitly told him. But still, I can be angry in my mind.

"What are you doing here?" I ask, standing as I strap my backpack over one shoulder, an equipment bag over the other, and juggle the Bluetooth speaker and choreography binder in my arms.

As if he hasn't verbally accosted me, told me off, and generally wanted nothing to do with his next-door neighbor, Everett slides the equipment bag off my shoulder and onto his while transferring the items in my arms to his own.

He's wearing a ball cap, which is so hometown sexy I can't help but bite my lip. Those green eyes look a little more lively than I've seen them, and somehow in October, his cheekbones are still dusted with a healthy tan. He looks like everything you hear in a country song, and I want to melt into him.

"You don't have to do that." My tone is all snotty annoyance.

"I know I don't." No other explanation than that, those eyes searing into mine.

We awkwardly stand there, because I know I'm supposed to direct him to my car where he can drop my things. But I don't know if I actually want him too. Or maybe I want him to do that *too* much, and that's why I hesitate.

"Just tell me where your car is, Kennedy." He rolls his eyes as he uses my full name.

I walk a fraction of a step in front of him as we both turn in the familiar direction of the parking lot. "So, why are you here?"

"I'm going to be a volunteer coach this season." Everett confirms what the other girls told me before practice.

It's the practical answer, but my question was deeper. Why even come over to me at all? Why are you carrying my things to the car?

Why hasn't my heartbeat returned to a normal rate since the moment I glimpsed you across the turf?

Homecoming is next weekend. The idea pops into my head as we walk under the banner hanging outside the stadium and our feet hit the parking lot pavement.

Now, I know he'll be at the game, that he'll watch as I walk out onto the field on the arm of one of the boys in the court. I found out three days ago that the voting swayed my way, that I am one of the four girls up for the honor of senior homecoming queen. I'm not modest enough to say I don't want it; deep down, every little girl dreams of wearing that tiara on her head.

Part of me foolishly hopes, is clinging to the idea, that he might ask me. No matter that Everett isn't even a student anymore, or that he's told me he basically wants nothing to do with me. I've dreamed for a long time about Everett Brock taking me to a school dance as his date. It never happened when he attended school here, and I spent both his junior and senior prom nights crying into my pillow. Like a moron.

Guess I'm still that same moron, because there's a lump in my throat imagining him slipping a corsage around my wrist. Of all the things I could be thinking right now, why does it have to be this?

"Homecoming seems like a fitting game for you to come home for. Local football legend back to coach our boys to victory?" The awkward giggle passes my lips before I can stop it. "I'm sure everyone will love having you back."

We brush up alongside my car, and I awkwardly fumble my keys out of my backpack. I can't make out the furrow in his brow as I turn to face him.

"You really shouldn't let yourself get so drunk at those barn parties. Anyone could have taken advantage of you." Everett's tone is snide, with a side of know-it-all.

There is so much to unpack as his advice blasts me in the face, I'm not sure where to start. When he first approached me at the end of practice, I thought maybe he was going to deliver an apology. For how he'd been treating me. Silly Kennedy, he just wants to further make you feel like shit.

All thoughts of sugarplums and kisses to a slow song on the cafeteria dance floor vanish.

My temper wins, getting the first word.

"Oh, because *you're* a choirboy," I sneer, rolling my eyes.

It's a terrible comeback, and I sound like a seven-year-old, but his prickly words caught me off guard and my first imperative is to protect my wounded heart.

"I'm not, but at least I don't pretend to be. I'm not running around here like the teacher's pet and everyone's best friends, then tossing back shots and trying to come out of my clothes."

I swear, if you looked at my cheek right now, it might bear Everett's handprint. That's how hard his words smack me.

My voice shakes with anger as I wrench my things away from him, my binder clattering to the ground. "You're a jerk! A really shitty, disgusting jerk!"

I can't even get a more coherent thought out there. One second, I'm thinking that Everett is coming to mend fences, to put us on a path back to friendship and maybe even something more. This is what I always do with him. I allow myself to get carried away with the Everett of my fantasies, rather than focus on the real guy standing right in front of me.

He shrugs, a smug grin on his lips. "I'm just trying to prevent you from being assaulted in the woods. Or becoming the next girl with a naked picture texted around the school."

Pain spreads through my heart like a rapidly moving bruise, and my fingernails dig into my palms. I'm always so quick to give him a chance, to forgive, to bend to the golden boy face and my damsel in distress thoughts. Everett's not going to save me, please, he barely wants to look at me. He doesn't now, and he didn't back then. If he really wanted me, he could have had me at any point. Even before he left for deployment, he kept me dangling on a string as a prospect, while I guarded my chastity like a warrior so that one day it could be his.

The things I wrote in that last letter, the one I should destroy after this encounter, my true feelings ... I'm so grateful he never saw it. That he was taken before it could get to him. I remember receiving it back, with Return to Sender stamped in big red letters on the envelope. It would only give him more fodder, more daggers to hurt me with.

I know better now. There was no us. There was no hope. I saw how easily he could turn on me. Finally, some common sense seems to have filtered through the trap he'd set up around my brain.

"You don't need to worry about me. In fact, I'm not even sure why you're talking to me. You've made it clear you have no interest in anything I do, Everett. So leave me alone."

"Leave you alone? Sheesh, that's what I've been trying to get you to do to me since I got here." He cracks, like we're having some kind of sarcastic rapport instead of his epic rejection of me.

"Just walk away. I'm done with this." Finally, I unlock my car and begin furiously shoving things in the back seat.

But Everett apparently hasn't drawn enough blood. "I just wouldn't want the future homecoming queen to end up puking her guts out on some guy's lap while—"

"ENOUGH!" I scream louder than the entire band practicing on an adjacent field.

Poking my finger into his chest, wishing it were a dagger, my voice takes on a scary low tone. "You may think you had me on some sort of string back in the day, but we're done with that now. You can't control me, drag me along like your puppet, and expect me to put up with all of this. I understand you've been through a lot, Everett. Honestly, I probably don't understand, which is why you hate me so much, right? It's my fault you were taken prisoner? Is that what you're going to blame me for next? Go ahead. I'm done caring what you think. You're the one who showed up where you knew I'd be. You're the one who followed me out here. What does that say about you?"

Blood whooshes in my ears, tears prick at the corner of my eyes, and my heart is going haywire. I barely register the look of shock on Everett's face, because I'm too busy scrambling my way into the driver's seat of my car.

Wrenching my seatbelt on and pushing the damn ignition button, I slam the door without waiting for him to speak.

What I told him is the truth. The strings he wrapped around my heart have finally snapped, tethering me to Everett no more.

13

I watch from the window as Kennedy and her girlfriends, and their dates, cheese away for the cameras.

Hands on each other's hips, making kissy faces for the photos, singing along to whatever god-awful pop song one of them is blaring from their phone speaker.

Just looking down on them, I feel myself glowering. I'm so far removed from the juvenile events of high school life that this all seems so trivial. And useless. And fucking fun. Just remembering my senior homecoming dance brings back some of the fondest memories—

Okay, fine. I'm jealous. But just a smidge. While I'm up here in my tower of solace, she's down there ready to have a fun night with friends and possibly drink some spiked punch.

Kennedy is also going to be crowned homecoming queen and dance with some dickhead. He'll wrap his hands around her waist, pull her close, all of that swishy maroon material bunching in his fingers ...

Fuck. That should be me.

She was in her cheerleading uniform last night when they crowned her senior homecoming queen at the football game.

That orange and white skirt hiked up just below her ass, her bright smile dazzling the crowd. On the arm of one of the players I've been coaching, she walked through the arch of balloons like her kingdom was receiving her.

Fuck, I hate how happy she is. It pisses me off, that someone who I used to be happy with, used to smile with, flirt with ... that she can still find joy in life when I'm so fucking miserable.

The hope in her eyes when I carried her things to the car after my first day of football coaching? I had to dash that. It was a stupid fucking idea to go up to her in the first place. But then she started babbling about homecoming, and I flashed back to the time Rachel told Scott who told some other guys I knew that Kennedy thought I'd ask her to be my senior prom date.

I'd wanted it to be her. I was a moron for not taking her. But I talked myself in and out of it so many times that, in the end, I just chickened out. Me, the future soldier, couldn't even muster the guts to ask the girl I was desperately infatuated with to prom.

But those memories came slamming back, and Kennedy had looked so fucking pretty in her practice uniform, and my cutting mouth went to work.

What I'd said was awful. I was the worst kind of prick, the kind who slut shamed a girl and rubbed false accusations in her face to soothe my bruised ego. My plan was to drive her away, to make her hurt as much as I did.

So why did I feel like shit for accomplishing what I'd set out to do?

It was because she called my bluff, fair and square. I'd expected to knock her on her ass, to level her with my verbal attack. But she'd spit back the same amount of realness, instead, devastating me. I'd been blaming her, blaming everyone around me, for the unspeakable atrocities that had happened to me. Even when they supported me, even when they tried to get through to me, even when Kennedy attempted to ... love me?

Did she love me?

I wonder if she's going with anyone, if a guy is meeting her at the dance. Of course, I know it's homecoming, I coached the game last night, and I could see Kennedy lingering after the final whistle blew. Did she expect me to ask her?

Fuck that, I'm far too old and far too cynical for high school dances anymore.

Maybe Logan Myers will end up being her date. The thought makes my blood boil, and I don't want it to but the fury is there, nonetheless.

I wanted to strangle the kid when he was making moon eyes at her during practice last week. The way he smugly pursued her, made her blush, chatted her up when he should have been focusing on the blocking drills we were doing.

It was all I could do to keep myself from running over there and tackling him around the middle, then marking my territory by peeing all over Kennedy. Gross metaphor, but you get the picture.

If I'm being honest, I want Kennedy. I still do. I always have. I've just never allowed myself to go there, didn't want to mess things up with my young boy ways if I wasn't ready. That's why I made her that promise, that's why I never allowed myself to get intimate with another girl. I've always been saving the special parts for her.

But now, I have no special left to give. If I was with Kennedy, there would be no romance. No sweet moments or love filled days. She would be miserably strapped to the shell of a guy who has little to no positivity left in the tank.

Still, it doesn't mean I want to see her with anyone else. I know that's selfish, and it makes me a complete asshole, but if I can't have her, no one else should either. The yearning and frustration eat me up inside, knowing that I can't make her happy but seeing her move on to someone else.

It takes all the willpower, and leg shaking, in me to stay shut up in my room rather than storm out of the house and down to the high school.

14

"Have a good night, guys."

I wiggle my fingers at Rach and Bianca, who giggle as Scott peels off into the night with Damien, Bianca's boyfriend, in the passenger seat.

They're probably all going to Bianca's house to make out, or more, in her basement. I was invited, but as the permanent fifth wheel, I just couldn't do it tonight. This night was special, second only to prom, and they should spend it romantically.

That's what I would have wanted if the person I'd always envisioned going to the homecoming dance with had ever asked me. All I got was one dance, my sophomore year.

I couldn't help but remember it periodically throughout the night. Everett had surprised me, sneaking up behind me just as the chords to John Legend's "All of Me" began to serenade the dance floor. His strong arms bolstered around me, my cheek on his chest, my fingers tangling in the dark blond curls at the nape of his neck.

When I was having a particularly rough day, if I missed him or even after we got the news about his death, I would imagine us back on that dance floor. The memory haunted me as I moved through the dressed-up cafeteria tonight, a cobweb stuck in my head that I was trying to swat away.

My heels are in my hands as I traipse up the driveway, drunk on ear-splitting music and too many hours goofily dancing with my friends. I'm not the type to spike the punch or take shots in the parking lot; I'm way too anxious to try to get tipsy for a school dance. Knowing me, I'd be the one to rat myself out to a chaperone because I couldn't take the pressure I was imagining from them.

The black heels clink against each other as I walk, the silk pleats of my dress swooshing against my legs. The night is cooler, and I didn't bring a coat or even a wrap, but I don't mind. After sweating against, and being sweat on, by hundreds of other teenagers, the breeze and nip are a welcome pair.

Tonight was more fun than I expected it to be. After the dark cloud Everett's return has painted over the last few weeks, it was nice to just enjoy a night of ridiculousness with my friends. We danced, laughed, tried to see who could rap the words to a Twista song the fastest, and just *had fun*.

Logan even asked me to slow dance, and I actually said yes. The senior tight end has always flirted with me, but until Rach and Bi suggested him, I never entertained the idea. I was waiting for a certain someone who I now know will never feel the same way about me. So, I decided it was time. When he held me in his arms as Ed Sheeran sang about perfection, I didn't have those enormous, all-consuming butterflies floating about in my gut. My skin didn't tingle, and I didn't get so nervous that I thought I might be sick. But, I was comfortable, and I felt admired when his eyes sparkled down at me, so I'm counting it as a good step in the right direction.

It's not until I'm halfway up my driveway that I hear him. I can't even see him, the darkness of the night shrouding me. My parents must have forgotten to turn on the lights above the garage, and the shadows hide the boy next door.

"You look beautiful." That deep voice sends goose bumps racing over my skin.

I jump, nearly out of my skin, still unable to see Everett but knowing it can't be anyone else spying on me.

"You scared the crap out of me. What are you even doing out here?" I ask, peering into the dark.

The figure steps into the moonlight, and goddamn it but my heart stutters. Even in athletic pants and a long sleeve, the boy next door steals my breath.

"Waiting for you." Those green eyes are so earnest.

The minute his voice hits the air, my bones sag with exhaustion. I'm so tired of this narrative, of the hot and cold.

"I'm over this, Everett. Pick on someone who actually cares." Sighing, I begin my ascent up the driveway.

"Where is your crown?" he asks, ignoring my declaration.

My back is to him, but I slow my steps. "I gave it to Ashley Tobin."

I hear the breath he blows out. "Kennedy, you were always too nice for any of us."

What I did, anyone would have done it. Ashley is a senior, has been in my grade since elementary school. We've been friendly since the day we met, and her having down syndrome just means I look out a little bit more for her than she does for me. We buddy up in clubs we both joined, and tonight, when she wanted to win homecoming queen, I gave her my crown.

"Funny, I thought that's something you apparently hate about me. Spare me the compassionate act tonight, Everett. I'm tired."

The moment my feet begin to move, his fingers lightly graze my elbow. Just the barest hint of a touch between us has my heart beating erratically, and every muscle south of my waist melting. How does he have that kind of power, and we've never so much as kissed?

"I owe you an apology. Several, actually. I'm sorry, Kennedy, so fucking sorry. I never should have said those things last week. Or the things I said before that. I was out of line, and none of it was even true. When I saw you tonight, with your friends—"

"You were spying on me?" I refuse to let the organ in my chest be charmed by him, but it's falling no matter what I internally yell at it.

"If you only knew how many times I've watched you through my window." His eyebrow hitches up.

"Pervert." A tiny smirk twitches at my lips.

"Come sit with me?" He extends a hand.

I don't take it, but I do step toward him. If I allow Everett to touch me right now, I know I won't stop it at that. Even for all of my talk, I'm so vulnerable when it comes to him. Case in point, I'm following him across the lawn and taking a seat next to him on the patio couch. The dark vibrates around us, and when I examine the back of both of our homes, all the lights are off.

"You look beautiful." He breathes, and even though we're not touching, I feel his words lick up my spine.

"You said that already." I almost hate myself for staying put.

"I carried that picture of you around in my uniform the entire time I was in that fucking sandstorm."

My heart flutters. "I forgot I sent that."

In one of the letters, I'd included this candid photo Rachel had taken of me at cheer practice. I'm in the middle of a laugh, my hair blowing behind my ears, and sun-kissed freckles dotting my nose.

"I never forgot one of your letters. Each of your lines tattooed onto my brain." Everett seems to be talking to himself more than to me.

And now my heart gallops, because he's feeding it the exact words it's always wanted to hear.

"You wrote a lot of things in those letters," I whisper.

"I meant every one of them." His response is so quick, I know its sincere. Everett didn't even have to think about it.

How can I allow him to do this every time? Take a perfectly good night, one I'd almost gone without thinking of him once, and completely turn it into the Everett show? I always let him, that's why. The charming things he's saying are invading my heart, twisting it against itself until it's convinced that it's not even a part of me. That it's ... *his*.

I think of Logan, of the easy, fun time we had tonight. I think of how simple the homecoming dance had been, how there wasn't a lump in my throat the whole time as I considered whether a certain boy would ask me to dance, or take someone else home.

"Or did you mean all the things you've said since you came home?" I cut my eyes to him.

From where we sit, our thighs almost touch. But it feels as if we're oceans apart, separated by the bodies of water that used to come between us when he was shipped overseas.

"You don't understand." Everett's expression pleads with me.

"No, I don't." I'm too tired to explain, to argue anymore.

"If I could, I would prove all the things I wrote to you. But that was another life. The things I've done ..."

He trails off and yet again, hides another piece of himself from me. I don't know what to say, or why I'm even still sitting here. The cold seeps in, making me shiver.

Everett must notice, because he shrugs out of his sweatshirt. The sleeves of his black tee underneath strain against his biceps, and my mouth goes dry as he leans over to envelop me in the warm material of his discarded layer. The sweatshirt smells like sandalwood and citrus, pure Everett.

"I'm sorry, Kennedy. For everything."

The whole sequence feels like a dream. I'm silent because I can't muster up a thought that won't end in my heartbreak. If I try to confess my feelings again, he'll only dash them, I know it. But if I forgive him for the things he's said, I'll also crack my chest wide open.

We sit on that patio for what feels like an eternity, both never saying all the emotions passing between our gazes.

"This is absolute bullshit."

I hear Dad swear into the phone, and I'm honestly shocked to my core. And not a lot stirs emotion in me these days. But my old man doesn't curse, and if he's doing so right now, it's because something is really pissing him off.

From where I lounge on the couch, as Mom starts dinner in the kitchen on the other side of our open concept house, I see him slam his cell down onto the table. The forks and glasses, which I set begrudgingly when Mom asked, rattle from the force.

"What's going on?" Mom asks, her voice brittle.

She's been jumpy and anxious since I got home. I know it's my fault, that what happened has probably changed her to the root, and for that I feel guilty.

"The goddamn military in this country is crooked. The whole lot of them!" Dad runs a shaking hand through his hair.

If they only knew.

"Dad, calm down." Even I'm concerned now, seeing him this fed up.

He blows out a breath. "I'm sorry. It's just … I don't how they can actively deny you your veteran benefits. Every time I call, it's a different excuse. Active investigation, paperwork being filed, some kind of active duty status still pending—"

"Are they going to send me back?" Until now, I hadn't really thought this was an option.

Because if that's so, I'll flee. I'll off myself. I will do anything to avoid going back to that sandstorm.

"No. You're staying right here. Anyone who tries that will have to come through me." I've never heard my father so fired up.

Taking a shaky breath, because it feels like a train hit my chest when he said active duty, I press my fingers against my temples. A headache is forming, and I need to hold it at bay.

The only reason Dad has been calling instead of me is because I won't muster the energy to do it myself. Not only do I want nothing to do with the Marines for the rest of my life, but talking to strangers and lobbying for myself isn't high on my list of priorities anymore.

"This is ridiculous. After what our son has been through ..." Mom breaks off, clamping her lips shut like she's trying not to let a sob out.

So, I'm captured by the enemy while serving my country and now they're going to try to deny me my veteran benefits? They're probably right to do that. If they knew what I'd done, what had really happened the night I was captured, they would do much worse than revoke my right to a free college education and the likes.

Not that I necessarily want the benefits. The therapy, the free education, the insurance, does any of it matter? I'm not planning on making something of my life, no matter how hard Dr. Liu or my parents try. What's done is done, I'm damaged goods.

"Let's all take a breath. There isn't more we can do about it now. I was lucky enough to pull your General's information out of the lowly desk guy this time, and I'll try to get in touch." Dad tries to move us past the tense moment.

"Everett, can you help me peel the potatoes?" Mom asks, taking his lead.

Huffing, I almost don't rise from the couch. But then I see their faces, and I know I can't disappoint them tonight. I've turned out to be such a letdown, such a loser, that I can do them this one small gratitude.

Joining Mom at the counter, I take the peeler from where she holds it out to me, and begin peeling the brown skins off the lumpy circles.

Looking across the yard, out the kitchen window past the red and orange leaves falling off the trees, I think about Kennedy. I shouldn't have gone over to her driveway last night. Shouldn't even have talked to her. In the harsh light of day, I only caused more trouble. Telling her she's beautiful, that I wish I could be with her? That was such a fucking mistake. In a moment of weakness, I let all the venom and vinegar leak out of me, revealing my true feelings.

But that can't be the Everett she knows now. I know what I did. I just strung her along even further. I gave her hope, and what a shitty thing to do. Because I can't act on it, I can't become the better guy. If Kennedy ever knew just what I've done, just what fucked-up things live inside my head?

She'd run for the hills.

They all would. If anyone knew what I was really capable of, they would send me straight back to that hole in the ground.

Still, there is something about her that is undeniable. I can't stay away.

Even though I know it's going to land us in a world of trouble, I can't fight the magnetic pull that brings us together time and again.

16

I reach the end of my sentence, slap a period on it, and should feel a floating sense of relief.

Except that all I feel is ... dissatisfied.

Looking at the six-hundred-word essay I have written, rewritten, tried to pour my heart and soul into, and had every emotion in between about, I feel no closure at all.

I thought that when I got to the end of compiling my thoughts, when my college admissions essay was done, that I'd feel some kind of elation. But I know that it's not done, it's not what I want to turn in. How does someone fit all of their hopes and dreams into three paragraphs of text? How do I relay just how much I yearn to go to my top choice, how much I want to study diligently and hone the craft of nursing? All of my sentences, my ideas, they sound so arbitrary and without emotion.

Staring at the screen, I frown until my temples hurt from all the negativity. I've been sitting in the Red Bird Coffee & Donut Shop for over two hours, on a Sunday no less, and it feels like I've accomplished nothing at all. Should I scrap it and start over again?

"Marble frosted still your favorite?"

A donut on one of the cafe's signature white and red striped plates appears in front of me. As does Everett Brock.

What the hell is he doing here? Did the Marines instill some kind of innate scent tracking in him that allows him to smell out my doubts and insecurities to pounce at the exact moment they're highest?

"I'd appreciate being left alone."

I don't answer his question, because yes that freaking flavor is still my favorite. But I won't let him see me internally drooling over it.

"You looked confused. Or maybe stuck. I thought a donut could help."

Do not look up into those clover-green eyes. Do not look up into those clover-green eyes.

Dammit, I cannot help it and I look up. Everett is smirking down at me, his broad shoulders filling out an old Brentwick Football long sleeve. He looks edible, and I want to slap my traitorous heart out of its droolfest.

"Thanks, but no thanks. I'm trying to concentrate." I do my best not to reach for that darn donut.

Cursing me out one day, telling me to stay away from him the next. Reeling me back in, telling me I'm beautiful. Now it's walking right up to me in the local coffee shop and planting my favorite donut in front of my face. It's like Everett is trying to win the Hot and Cold Contest of the Millennium and winning by a landslide.

Despite my attempt to shrug him off, the legs of the chair on the opposite side of my table scratch against the linoleum as he pulls it out to sit.

"I'm trying to work, Everett." Though really, I should welcome the distraction with open arms.

Talking to my childhood crush, and current love interest, is way better than failing through my college admissions essay.

Everett slaps down his book, and I read the title as the large anthology lands across the table. *Brentwick Community College Course Guide.*

"So you can work, I can circle which of these courses won't make me want to blow my brains out." Everett wiggles an eyebrow at me, though I don't think his choice of words are particularly funny.

"You're going to community college?" Ironic that we're both struggling with the institution of higher education.

He shrugs, and I notice him set an Oreo chocolate donut and a large coffee down next to the syllabus. We've both had the same order since we hit high school, coming in to the Red Bird for "coffee chats" to feel like grown-ups. When there isn't much in the way of adventure or excitement in a town for people under the age of twenty-one, we found the hang out spots we could.

He shrugs, and I trace his jawline with my gaze. "Figure I don't have much else to do. And I need to make some money if I ever want to get out of my parent's house."

A wave of unease goes through me. "Well, you've only been home for a couple of months. Don't you think it's nice to be home with your parents? I'm sure they love having you there."

I also don't know if Everett is equipped to handle living by himself. From what I've seen, when he isn't lashing out at me, he shuts himself up in his room. He barely leaves the house, and I have a feeling he's been going through some massive PTSD from what he went through.

Everett scowls, picks up his donut, and takes a large bite. I shouldn't eat his apology treat, but the marble frosted looks too appetizing sitting there, and so I do the same. Christ, it's so good.

"I'm a twenty-something veteran living underneath his

parent's roof. They're constantly checking up on me, invading my privacy, and I feel like I can't breathe. Does that sound like a great situation?"

"Well, I guess not, but where would you live?"

"An apartment. Maybe I'd move. Who knows."

Ah, the hot and cold is back in action. Cue Indifferent Everett, the guy who just brought me a donut to apologize and is now telling me he'd like to move away from me and everyone he loves.

"I think community college is a great start, though. And your assistant coaching gig. They probably make you feel ..." I trail off, because I was going to say normal and that's such an asshole thing to say.

"You were going to say normal, weren't you?" Everett smirks, but I don't miss the way his jaw tics.

"No," I lie and shove another piece of marble frosted in my mouth.

"What are you working on?" Everett turns my laptop to him before I can stop the motion.

"Hey!" I throw my hands up to cover the screen, like I'm some kind of pre-teen guarding her secret diary.

He peeks through my fingers and even moves one so he can read the screen better. The ounce of contact, that one innocent touch, sends shock waves through the air between us.

"Your college essay? You haven't submitted it yet? It's almost ... is the deadline this week?" How he knows so much about college admissions when he never applied himself astounds me.

A grimace works its way over my face. "Just making some last-minute changes to make it perfect."

Everett studies my face. "No, you're not. You don't like it. That's why you haven't turned it in yet."

How the hell does he know me this well, even after all this time.

I sigh, relenting. "No, I'm not. I don't like it. I can't seem to get it right. How am I supposed to fit everything I feel, all of my personality, into these faceless paragraphs? They're going to hate me, they won't understand my passion or—"

Everett snorts, and I stop, rearing back. He was baiting me, waiting for me to admit an insecurity and now, like I predicted, he'll pounce on it.

"Kennedy, no one could ever hate you. You're the most quali-fied person I've ever met, no matter what it is you're trying to achieve, and anyone would be an utter moron to deny you of it. I'm sure this essay is light-years better than what every other kid is writing theirs about. You just have these impossible standards, even for yourself."

That last part feels like a backhanded compliment, but my heart is beating so hard and my cheeks are so flushed right now that I can't even acknowledge the barb. I think Everett just told me I was great. In a sense. Maybe.

"It just doesn't feel like me. And it's too late to do anything about it." I shrug, trying to seem nonchalant.

"Can I read it?" he asks, with a note of hope I haven't heard in his voice since he came home.

"No." I say it so quickly that I curse myself.

Because the curious light immediately goes out of Everett's eyes.

"I just mean ... the topic is a little private." How can I let him read my essay about not being able to cope with death when he's seen so much of it?

He nods slowly, taking a sip of coffee. "I get it. But again, I'm sure it's the best fucking college essay I've ever not read."

"Everett!" I squeak, because the people two tables over heard him drop the *F* word and are now looking at us.

"Come on, Kennedy, you aren't afraid of a little curse word. I've seen you throw around worse three beers in." He rolls his eyes, the grin marking his lips purely devilish.

That makes me laugh, because I've been known to rap while drunk. "If you can't spit a little Cardi B once in a while ..."

We both look at each other, exchanging smiles in the silence. It's the first time since he's been home that I feel like us again. The Kennedy and Everett we used to be; friendly, known to make each other laugh, with an underlying chemistry that can't be denied. For a split second, his capture and return, the promises and terrible words, they cease to exist. I have a glimpse of what we could have been, and if I'm being truthful, what I still want us to be.

"So, can I sit here and look through my course catalogue, or are you going to keep trying to distract me?" His lopsided grin has me mesmerized.

I roll my eyes, but we both know I'd never tell him to leave.

"You can stay. But be quiet. And maybe buy me another donut."

17

EVERETT

T he first letter I ever wrote to Kennedy was on enemy territory.

I was deployed only weeks after bootcamp ended, sent to the front lines as one of the Marines black ops recruits. I was high on the adrenaline of a naïve soldier's heart and also scared shitless. As I lay awake, listening for the sounds of enemy footsteps or bullets whizzing past my head, I'd take out a piece of paper and scrawl my feelings and thoughts by moonlight.

I told her, in that first correspondence, that I missed her. That one of my biggest regrets was not kissing her before I left. Those are the types of things you say when you're thousands of miles away and feeling like a big shot who might have his head blown off at any moment. I told Kennedy about my training, what little I could divulge, and I wrote about missing our coffee shop dates and barn parties and ...

Her.

I wrote some things in those letters that I honestly didn't feel like, at the time, I'd ever have to face. Those are the things you do when you feel like your life was in the balance. Yes, I was cocky enough to think I was coming home. But I was also cocky enough to think that I wouldn't have to have a real conversation about the letters we exchanged.

Kennedy and I wrote to each other for a year, sometimes I'd send multiple or receive multiple ones a week. Her curvy, scrawled handwriting was my comfort at the end of a long day. Her words gave me strength when I didn't think I could get through another patrol. I carried her picture in my back pocket through every terrifying mission.

It's easy to forget that, to ignore the stack of letters still in my canvas recruit bag that I haven't dared to open. It's easy to ignore the promises I made her, simply because I don't want to deal with the consequences of making them. Blaming the conversation I don't want to have on my PTSD, on the torture I suffered, it's a cheap excuse. But one I thought I could use.

Now, I'm not so sure. We sat across from each other in that coffee shop for an hour or two. The quiet companionship, the crackling heat of sexual tension, the glances we both stole when we thought the other wasn't looking.

I can't ignore that anymore.

Something is shifting with us, something I can't stop or control. The more I'm around Kennedy, the more I want to bring up the kiss I never gave her. The date I never took her on. The Valentine's Day I never planned. All of these were things in my letters, and even though I've fought hard against my feelings, they're stronger than my willpower.

I've been lying on my bed, staring at the ceiling, thinking about taking her letters out of my bag for almost an hour. Will they cause me pain? Cause me to be transported back to a time when all hope in my body was crushed, along with my bones? Or will they give me hope, and perhaps courage, to finally tell her how I feel?

Kennedy's light comes on, the twinkle of it drawing me to my own window.

How many times has the flick of illumination from her side caught my attention? I've stared across the void of our houses hundreds of times. At first, as a shithead teen trying to get a peepshow. The only thing I ever managed to see was Kennedy dancing around in her training bra, a memory that I used thousands of time back then to jerk of to. If she knew about that now, she'd probably smack me.

But later, when we both got into high school and my feelings for her ran deeper, it was more of a study. I wanted to know her, wanted to read her expressions, see who she was when no one was looking. I've seen Kennedy thoughtful, I've seen her sad. I've heard her humming old show tunes through the window when it was open on a summer night.

Now, I linger in the shadows of my room, standing right in front of the window but all the same holding my breath. I've wanted to storm down her door since yesterday, to finally give her that kiss I promised years ago.

She walks to the window, her slender yet curvy body swelling in all the right places. Backlit from the lamp on her desk, I can make out her figure but not the specific parts of her body. When she comes closer to the window, moving until the moonlight streaks over her face, she's looking straight at me. Those coffee-colored eyes hold mine, questioning, searching.

I lean an arm against the window jamb, pressing my body closer, as I feel my cock harden. My sweatpants begin to tent, all from just watching her through this pane of glass. Like some kind of voyeur, in this secret, taboo way that only she and I are privy to. Can she tell how much she's turning me on?

Kennedy holds my stare, her chest rising and falling in rapid succession. Is she wet under those jeans? Do her panties hold evidence of what I do to her? Of all the things I wished for when I thought I was about to die, making love to Kennedy Dover was at the top of the list.

I could go over there, invite myself in. Or better yet, scale the tree outside her room. She'd let me in, we both know that. My heart thrums against the bones containing it, the need to reach down and tug on my cock so primal that I nearly do.

But holding off somehow seems more illicit. As if I need her permission. As if I'm daring her to reveal all of that pretty olive skin to me.

She lets her hair down first, pulling it from its tie, and the waves of dark chocolate hair fall over her shoulders. The material of her sweater looks soft, a creamy pale pink, and I can see the way her jeans hug her hips.

Pressing closer, I nod my chin, giving her the signal to keep going. Her hands fall to the hem of her sweater, pulling it up and over her head. My heart stops, sputtering in my chest, and then falls a little when she reveals the lacy tank top underneath.

The skinny straps of the top slip, one plunging down her arm, and I wish so desperately I could kiss her bare shoulder. I watch as Kennedy skims her fingers up her arm, putting it back in place, and then brushing her hair over so it falls down her back. The swell of her cleavage draws my eyes, rising and falling in time with her breathing.

"*Take it off*," I mouth, the sound silent to even my own ears.

Kennedy quirks an eyebrow, not ashamed or embarrassed, but almost challenging me. As if to say, "*How far are we going to take this?*"

I'm not sure how it escalated to this. Maybe we need an entire property and panes of glass between us to get to the root of our mutual lust.

Beats pass, and I blow out a breath I didn't realize I was holding. We're suspended here, waiting to see if she'll give in to my dare.

I must blink, because I miss the beginning of her arms descent, but in the next second, Kennedy is pulling the scrap of material over her head. Creamy expanses of skin, her tight little waist and taut stomach are exposed. The dangerous flirting of her jeans, taunting me from across the gap, stay firmly buttoned and in place.

My eyes skim up, capturing and memorizing each inch of her. The curve of her ribs, the swell of her breasts, the lacy white bra pushing them up. Fuck, do I wish I could see her nipples, reach out my tongue to lick one. My hands itch to touch her, to mold her tits in my palms.

When I finally reach her face, the flush of her cheeks only serves to turn me on more. Kennedy reaches her arms out, grasping the curtains on either side. I want her to close them, and at the same time, it will drive me fucking mad if she does.

With a final smirk, a small smile of victory, she slowly pulls them shut, pausing for a beat to give me one last look at her.

A second ticks by, and then another. I stay pressed there, my hips involuntarily flexing, seeking Kennedy's presence at the window once more. But she isn't coming back, I've seen all I'm allowed to tonight. My heart still hammers in my chest, the head of my cock twitches with the need for release.

There is only one option, and soon, my body hits my bed as my hand seeks the steel pipe in my pants. I wrap my fist around myself, tugging and a growl emits low in my throat. In my mind, Kennedy is on top of me, molding her body to mine. My hands skim down her curves, tugging at each nip of her waist, feeling the velvet of her skin beneath my fingertips.

As she grinds herself on me, I pull down the cups of her bra, finally seeking the tight budded nipples I want between my teeth. Suddenly, she slinks down my body, taking control as she pulls down the band of my sweats.

Jerking faster, tugging hard at my tip until my vision goes white at the edges, I imagine Kennedy sinking her mouth down onto me, and—

I'm coming, hot streaks jetting out into my boxers. Orgasmic bliss hurtles down my spine, ricocheting through my body as I gasp to remain conscious.

My breath comes out in labored puffs, the exertion of my climax so heady that I fear I might fall over if I try to stand up. It's the first time I've truly allowed myself to fantasize about Kennedy since I've been home.

And being a twenty-year-old virgin doesn't help.

With the desire that just engulfed my body attended to, and no more tantalizing flirting out the window, I'm left feeling well, bored.

My duffel bag taunts me, the canvas suitcase shoved into a corner of my room. When my mom first brought it up, about a week after I came home, I was shocked. I thought that thing had disappeared somewhere in the desert around the same time I did. I learned that my platoon sent it back to my parents when they assumed I was dead, along with the scant number of items I'd left at base camp.

I know they're in there, her letters. They were some of the only personal items I kept in my bunk, so I'm sure they were sent home to my grieving family.

Suddenly, I can't wait to dig into them. I jump up, a wave of frantic energy moving over me. I'm so hot and cold these days, I don't know whether to cover myself in clothing or run naked into the freezing cold.

Rifling through the bag, the scent of the desert and military life hits me so hard that I almost keel over. But I persist, wanting to find those letters. My hand lands on what feels very close to paper, and I grab, pulling it out.

Lo-and-behold, the bundle of letters from Kennedy, tied up with some twine someone must have found. My fingertips shake as they pull the makeshift bow off the letters, and Kennedy's handwriting with my overseas address smiles up at me.

Taking the first one from the pile, I notice it's unopened.

She was writing me after I was taken prisoner. The thought hits me like a ton of bricks, because until this moment I truly haven't thought about what it was like for everyone here, waiting to hear if I was dead or alive.

I open it, wrapping past the seal of the envelope and unfolding the worn paper inside.

Everett,

I haven't gotten a letter in nearly two weeks. I'm trying to hold out hope that you're just on a mission, because the other option is so fear inducing, it brings me to my knees just thinking about it.

I hope you're safe, and that you're fighting bravely just like I know you've always planned to. We all miss you so much, it hurts. I miss you. I wish things had been different before you left, that all the things we've written to each other in the past year could have happened before—

I have to stop reading. The memories this is conjuring, the thought of where I was while she was writing this letter, shipping it to me, it's agony. She missed me. Kennedy missed me.

And now I'm back, just yards away from her bedroom window, and we still can't make it work.

"*Copy, responding to scene now.*"

The radio crackles next to me as I lower the volume, shooting a guilty, apologetic look at Rach and Bi. "Sorry."

Rach huffs while Bi rubs my shoulder, excusing the loud noise.

"We're trying to concentrate here. How can we possibly adore KJ Apa's abs with that medical squawking going on?" Rach asks, but turns back to the screen.

We've been binging *Riverdale* on Sunday nights, since none of us got into the teen high school drama when it first came out. Personally, I'm much more of a Netflix murder documentary kind of girl, but the death and mystery on this show keeps me interested while my best friends drool over the quintessential hot guys.

But attending the watchathon comes with strings for me tonight. I warned Bianca before I got to her house that my EMT radio would be in tow, though I'm not sure Rachel really loves my dedication.

I'm on call tonight, meaning I can stay home or hang out

with friends, but the likelihood of me getting dispatched to a scene or an emergency is higher than the nights I'm deemed off duty. Brentwick isn't a small town, and Judy and some others are full time, salaried EMTs, but there have been a few occurrences of needing more hands. I'm happy to do it, after all it's my passion and more hands-on experience means more preparation for nursing school.

"I'm glad they recast Reggie, because Charles Melton is a freaking smoke show," Bianca comments.

I nod. "I can't disagree. Those lips, mmm."

He really is a beautiful man. And I'm glad I can take a night away from the stress I've been inflicting on myself. It seems like, for the first marking period of the school year, I've been so worried about college admissions, the cheer squad ... Everett.

When I finally clicked submit on my college apps, which went out to the four schools I'm applying to, I sat in my room and stared at the walls. It's as if I should have felt something ... more? I've been waiting a long time to start the college chapter of my life. Not because my high school life or childhood was terrible, it's quite the opposite actually. I just think that college is going to be the time I thrive, where my peers mature to the level I've always felt I operated at.

Maybe then, I won't feel as grown up and boring as everyone jokes that I am. Maybe during college, I'll finally be able to focus on the things I really want to accomplish, in a real way.

"God, imagine those lips on your body? I would sell my right tit." Bianca sighs dreamily.

I snort. "You'd sell your boob to kiss Charles Melton? What happens when he sees you without one boob?"

"We'd figure that out later." She shrugs.

Rachel texts furiously, smirking at her phone.

"Who are you talking to?" I ask, though I already know the answer.

"Scott. This show makes me horny with all the pent-up sexual tension. I need to get laid." She sticks out her tongue at me.

"Gross. I don't need your pheromones stinking up the room." I pretend to make a disgusted face.

"Doesn't it though? You just know everyone on this cast is boning each other." Bianca nods rapidly.

I can't say I disagree. There does seem to be some cloud of lust floating over every scene.

"How do you know when you're ready to, um, lose it?" I pose the question, unable to look at my friends.

There is a moment of silence before they dissolve into a fit of hysterics and "OH MY GOD's!"

"Are you telling me you want to have sex? With who? Logan?" Rachel jumps up and down on the legs folded under her, and Bianca quickly pauses the show.

I should confess to my best friends about what happened the other night with Everett, but it feels like a secret I want to keep just for him and me. They don't know yet, because I haven't spilled the tea, about how we've been connecting the past week or so. How all the animosity seems to have drained from our relationship, and things were getting extremely ... steamy.

I can't believe I almost did a striptease for Everett through our windows. The guy hasn't even followed through on his promise to kiss me, and here I am showing him my bra.

What's worse is that I'm ashamed I chickened out. Would another girl, a more experienced girl, given him the whole package? Should I have crooked my finger and told him to come over?

What happened feels like a sacred moment, this scorching hot event that I haven't been able to stop thinking about since. Every time I picture him, his eyes ablaze and his pants tented from his erection, my whole body goes into a full flush of heat.

"Let's say that hypothetically, yes." What they don't know, they can't gossip about.

And I'd rather have them bugging me about my nonexistent chemistry with Logan Myers, rather than pressuring me about my very real feelings for Everett.

"Well, you should probably get on the pill first and foremost." Bianca comes out of left field with this very mature contribution.

"Oh." I hadn't even considered it. "I probably should."

Was I really considering having sex with Everett? After the night at our windows, yes. I know that if he wanted to, I would in a heartbeat. It has always been him, and if he's ready, I am more than so.

"Definitely need the pill. And I can lend you some condoms if you don't have a box yet. The guy should usually supply, but you can never be too careful," Rachel instructs.

"What if he's been with someone else? I'm so inexperienced."

"Logan? From what I hear on the gossip wire, he's a virgin." Rachel looks at me, perplexed.

"Well, you never know," I sputter, covering for myself.

Because more than likely, hell, most definitely, Everett is not a virgin. I'm sure he's been with countless other girls, most of them probably gorgeous and college-aged.

Bianca shrugs. "Most guys think deflowering a virgin is a turn on, so you don't have to worry there. Aside from that, just follow his lead. Trust me, Kenny, once you get in the mood, it's kind of second nature to know what to do. And when you don't, just go with what feels good. And talk. God, guys love it when you talk. That way, you'll know what makes them feel good."

"Right? Like with blow jobs, Scott loves when I ask him questions. Or when I dirty talk, sometimes we fantasize that he's my teacher—"

"*Okay*! I'm going to stop you right there," I interrupt Rachel's TMI session.

I really wish that, at this exact moment, a call would come in for me to go to work. I would rather go to the scene of a car accident than sit here and be grilled with questions about doing the horizontal hula with a guy. My question is coming back to bite me in the ass.

"I think I've got the basics, thanks, guys." Throwing my palms up to them, I signal that it's more than enough information for one night.

Bianca leans over where she has been lounging on the couch, throwing her arms around me.

"Whenever you decide it's time, I hope you choose the right person."

Something in her eyes when she pulls back tells me she knew all along that I wasn't talking about Logan.

Six teenagers sit in a booth at the local diner.

The three boys wear their dirty football jerseys over jeans, a silent boast about how hard they fought for the victory tonight. The girls sit under their wings, cheerleading sweatshirts covering their short skirts, their slim legs pebbled from standing in the cold for so long.

From an outsider's point of view, we look like a group of yuppy, popular jocks and their girlfriends. I guess it's not far off.

The only thing they wouldn't realize is that I'm trying to force my heart to be invested in the guy sitting next to me, rather than pine after the one I can never be with.

"One time, Scott did the entire omelet challenge in an hour," Logan spills.

Rachel turns to him, astonished. "When was this? Surely, not when we were dating. I would have never touched you if you'd eaten upward of three dozen eggs, *Gaston*."

"Oh my God, Rach!" Bianca giggles at the clear bathroom situation Rachel is trying to allude to.

"Nope. It was freshman year, and I was a fucking champ.

Puked like twenty minutes after, but my picture is over on the wall." Scott brushes his shoulder off and then points to the wall behind the cash register.

We've been at the diner for about an hour, noshing on apps and different sandwiches after the football team won their game tonight. The entire restaurant is full of students from our high school, six or seven people crammed into every booth, with parents and coaches present too. It's the local hot spot after every game, whether it be football in the fall or baseball in the spring.

"Would you ever do one of those challenges?" I ask Logan, simply to start a conversation.

"I think I probably would, but I'd need a good incentive. Free meals from the restaurant, or money. I would not scarf down fifty buffalo wings for a T-shirt."

I laugh, trying to imagine sitting in front of fifty chicken wings and voluntarily eating them all. "No, I guess I wouldn't either."

"What kind of food could you eat like that? Just scarf it all down?" Rachel muses to us all.

"Ice cream, hands down. Any flavor, but it's just so good." Bianca nods sagely.

"Pizza, for sure." Logan winks at me.

"Burgers, I could eat thousands of those little ones at White Castle," Damien, Bianca's boyfriend says.

"Sushi. One hundred percent, I could eat sushi all day long." Rachel crosses her arms over her chest.

"Bullshit," Bianca and Scott say at the same time, and then laugh at each other.

"You'd get sick of it after the second spicy tuna roll," I agree, shivering just thinking about that much sushi.

"All right, smarty pants. What food would you eat for twenty-four hours straight?" Rachel snips at me.

Tapping my chin, I ponder the question. "French fries."

"That's not a food challenge food!" Logan laughs, his forehead hitting my shoulder from where he sits next to me.

It's an intimate gesture, one a boy who likes a girl flawlessly executes to make it look nonchalant but really he wants to touch her.

"Is too! I could eat fries all day long!" I argue, while the others around the table burst out laughing and shake their heads like I'm wrong.

"Fries isn't a challenge food. It has to be something substantial. That's a side, not a main." Scott tries to act high and mighty.

"He's right," Bianca says, while Rachel backs her up. "Yep."

I pout, only half-faking my annoyance. "Who made you all the authority on food challenges? I can fantasize about my ideal food challenge food and you can have yours. Leave me be!"

Pushing at Logan, who is still trying to get close to me by half slumping an arm around my shoulders, I huff.

"Aw, come on, Kennedy. We're just teasing."

When I turn my head to look at him, his lips are so close to mine, I have to suck in a breath. That should make my heart jump, the fact that a seriously cute boy is so close to kissing me. But I feel nothing.

The jingle of the bell over the door grabs my attention, and for good reason, as if I could sense him. When I turn, Everett is walking up the same aisle of the restaurant our booth is in, two of the other assistant football coaches behind him.

Immediately, his eyes find me. Search my expression and then flit to where Logan sits beside me.

Logan's varsity jacket hangs around my shoulders, the orange and white leather marking me as his for everyone to see. He offered it to me because it's a bit cold in here, but I'm not dumb enough not to notice the looks everyone is giving us as they pass to their tables. When a boy gives a girl his football letter, it's significant.

I haven't seen Everett since the night in our rooms, when he watched me with the heat of a thousand suns. But now that I'm here, in his crosshairs, those gorgeous eyes roving over my face ...

My skin feels like it's burning up. Fire licks up my thighs, spine, arms, blazing a path to my heart that beats irregularly. For a moment, we're the only two people in the room. He's the only boy to ever see me so vulnerable, so exposed. I gave that to him, a secret we now share.

This is what I crave, this is the way it should feel when the most gorgeous man you've ever seen walks into a room. I'm sitting with Logan's jacket and arm around my shoulder, and my heart couldn't care less. But Everett Brock so much as looks at me, and I'm a pool of lust at his feet.

"Kennedy," he says, his tone and expression so cold he could freeze ice.

"Coach! So freaking funny I call you coach now—" Scott starts up, putting his hand up to fist pound Everett, but something cuts him off.

Without warning, Everett leans over the booth, uses one of those callused, strong hands to grip my jaw, and plants a kiss on my lips.

Right there, in front of everyone.

I'm so stunned, so caught off guard, that the squeak from my lips echoes down Everett's throat. He moves his mouth, just a fraction, so that our lips slide in tandem. Liquid heat throttles down my spine, and my eyes flutter closed. I don't feel my body, the only thing that exists are his lips on mine.

This is the kiss I've been waiting for since I was a little girl, and—

Someone coughs, bringing me back to reality, and I shove hard at Everett's chest.

"What the hell!" Comes out of my mouth at the same time Logan jumps up and shouts, "What the fuck, bro?"

My cheeks are a shade of red I don't even want to see in a mirror right now, shame and anger mixing with the embarrassment. Everett looks stunned, but smug, and I climb over a gaping Rachel as I go for him. I may be tiny in comparison with the former soldier, but he doesn't resist as I damn near drag him out of the diner without a backward word to my friends.

Somewhere in the scuffle, Logan's varsity jacket slips off my shoulders, so when we break through the exit to the diner and out into the cold, I'm shivering in my thin cotton long sleeve and cheerleading vest.

"What the hell was that?" I spit, rage making the shivers quake even harder.

Everett runs a hand through his hair, but fire burns in his eyes. "If you think I'm going to sit back and watch while he puts his hands all over you—"

"He wasn't putting his hands all over me!" I shout back.

"You had his goddamn varsity jacket slung over your shoulders. We both know what that means, Kennedy." Everett's finger comes in, pointing at me, accusing me.

I'm so exasperated, I can barely get my thoughts together, though I try. "So what? You don't even know what that was because you didn't bother to ask, not that you've staked any claim. You don't want me, remember? Besides all that, you think that was a good way to stop what might or might not be happening between Logan and me? Stealing our very first kiss in the freaking diner in front of everyone?"

His body is strung tight, every muscle bulging with barely-held restraint. "Yeah, maybe it was a good plan. Got you out here with me, didn't it?"

Everett wears a smug, shit-eating grin that I want to punch off his jaw.

"Here I was, thinking you were actually changing. That we'd come to some sort of truce. I thought I saw a glimpse of the guy I used to know. But you're still that angry, shell of a man who returned to Brentwick. You promised me a kiss, you promised me so much that you've never followed through on. That was it. Our first kiss. Out of a moment of spite. In all the times I ever dreamed about it, that would have never been the circumstance I picked. Hell, I wish I could erase that moment, make it like it never happened. That's not the kiss I wanted."

"Guess I'm not the man you wanted, then."

"I guess not." My voice is dangerously close to breaking.

I whip around, not wanting him to see the tears I'm about to let loose.

"Wait, Kennedy, I-I didn't mean to. FUCK! I'm such an idiot—"

When I turn back around, rage singeing my veins, Everett is pale and his are eyes full of fear.

"You didn't mean to kiss me? You didn't mean to do it in front of people? What, Everett? Is there more you'd like to sling at me? Have you not torn me down enough?" I go into attack mode.

And immediately, the one shred of humanity I saw tonight is locked up tight, disappearing from his eyes.

"You got it, your fucking kiss. Now can you stop whining about it. It wasn't good for you? Well, it was a hell of a lot crappier for me. So much for all the pomp and circumstance leading up to it. Now we can both move on knowing there was nothing there anyway."

His words cut so deep, I'm surprised I'm not bleeding when my eyes drop to the pavement.

That's the thing, though. There was so much emotion, so much confirmation of what we could be, packed into that kiss.

Into that stupid, public, spiteful, half-a-second kiss that shouldn't even be allowed on the tally board.

That I have to wonder what would it be like if our lips really met in the way we've always deserved?

D roplets of wetness from the pavement hit the back of my calves, the cold darkness surrounding me as my legs pump.

When I could no longer stand the sound of my own thoughts, shut up in my room once more, I decided to come out and exhaust myself physically. Maybe if I run a full fucking marathon, I'll be able to pass out.

Though my body, limbs and muscles have been put through the ringer, they miraculously healed with little disability. Every time my left foot hits the roads of Brentwick, my ankle cracks. There is a lag in the fingers on my right hand, from being crushed under the weight of a brick in my hole. My right knee also aches for days at a time, where a bullet was shot clean through the flesh. Thankfully, my kneecap was intact, because with broken bones like that, I probably would have died.

So I'm able to run, now that I've returned to normal life. My lungs burn with the frigid air pumping in and out of them, and the dark streets of my hometown close in around me. I'm so fucking pissed at myself, at the predicament I've landed in, that I want to drown it out with the death metal screaming in my ears.

A fucking idiot, that's what I am for doing what I did at the diner the other night. I'm not sure what came over me, but I saw red when I spotted Logan and Kennedy in that booth. I wanted to drag her out of there, over my shoulder again. She is mine, even if we've been doing this dance around each other, circling closer and closer.

But I shouldn't have kissed her like *that*. I wasted it, our first kiss, on an angry whim. I was so numb, so reactive, that I spoiled the one thing I'd been promising her for years. The kiss wasn't even particularly good, though that hadn't stopped the sparks crackling between us. And the raw, primal feeling in my gut that it would be the kiss to end all kisses.

No, it should have been special. After I'd taken her on a date, or in a field of fucking fireflies or some shit. Instead, the scent of overdone hamburgers and Logan Myers's sweaty football jersey tainted the whole thing. So yeah, I'm an idiot, and that moment is one we'll never get back.

I've been running for probably an hour, not counting the miles or minutes, but my innate sense of time calculated to a science. It's way past the time when anyone would be out here, maybe close to midnight, so when I get to Main Street, I know what I'm headed for before my feet even process where they're taking me.

I come to a dead halt when I spot it, my own face taunting me from above the square that houses the most popular staple stores and restaurants in town. At my ankle, my knife calls to me, held in the strap that I haven't been able to take off since I got home. If someone ever comes for me again, I'll be ready.

The banner hangs above the town square, my face plastered on one side, the words *Brentwick's Real Life Hero, Welcome Home Corporal Everett Brock, next to it*.

They're lies, each and every word. I'm no hero, especially not for the people of this town. I never earned that corporal title, it was honorarily given to me because of my many months in captivity. And it was all fucking bullshit.

The reason I got captured, the real reason my unit was in the place we were in. If anyone in this town knew that, they'd call me a traitor and a murderer. Rage suffuses my blood, and I'm ready to rip out someone's throat, but I'll settle for the next best thing.

Luckily, my military muscles still work like they're supposed to, and I shimmy up the light pole, until I reach where the banner is tied. Pulling my knife from its holster, I cut into the twine, releasing the lying banner from its prominence above the square. It flutters down, landing on the wet pavement still damp from this afternoon's rain.

My sneakers hit the sidewalk, and I stomp to it, grabbing a fistful of banner and stabbing my knife through it. As I cut, my hand shaking as I pull jagged edge after jagged edge, the fury seeps from my bones into the knife. Slicing through every piece of my personality that people believe they know.

"What are you doing?"

Someone hisses behind me, and I stop, my knife paused in the banner as it divides my face down to the nose. I know the voice, because of course, she's here to witness this. To see just one more of my failings as a man, as a rational human.

Turning slowly as I push the blade of my army knife back into its handle, Kennedy stands on the street. Her eyes are wide as her jaw hangs open. She's in her EMT uniform, one I've never seen her wear since I wasn't here when she got certified.

"Doing this town a favor. This banner is bullshit." I point to it, as if the banner ruined my entire day.

Which, it kind of did.

"Everett, it's not. This town is so proud of you." Her eyes flicker, looking sideways, as if she can't address me directly.

God, she's such a good person. Even with what I did, with how mad she must be at me, she's calling me a hero.

"Well, they shouldn't be. I'm fucked up." My voice raises a notch.

"You've been through something traumatic, but it doesn't mean you have to be *dramatic*. You served your country. Your town wants to honor that."

Did she just call me dramatic? Inside, my blood begins to boil. Because Kennedy, with her perfect fucking life, can't understand just how tragic mine is.

"You just can't stand that the world isn't this orderly, perfect thing that you can mold if you just work hard enough. Everything you've ever touched turns to gold in your hands. If you can dream it up in your little diary, then it must come true. Princess wishes and all! Boo fucking hoo, Kennedy. The world fucking chews you up and spits you out, limbs broken and dreams stabbed through the fucking heart."

"But you said, in your letter ..."

"Forget the fucking letter, Kennedy. Jesus, you're like a desperate child. Do you not understand that nothing is the way it was? I'm not fulfilling school kid promises, or chasing crushes like it's some freshman year football game! Grow the fuck up, this is the real world. People lie, they disappointment you, and love is a fucking sham! You have no idea what I'm capable of. Or what evils the world holds."

I've said too much, and I stalk away before I betray my secret even more. If I tell her, I'm not sure I could protect her. If anyone ever found out that I slipped up, that I revealed something to her ...

Not only that, but the talk of our letters unnerves me. There is a letter in the bundle, one of mine that was never sent. It's the one that contains too many of my feelings, that betrays too much of how deeply I care about her. In the light of day, I think I can handle this thing between Kennedy and me. That I can live a normal life, overcome my demons, love a person as they should be loved.

But it's when the darkness sinks in that I know the truth. I'm not a normal person, I never will be again. What happened to me, what I've been put through, it chemically alters a part of your soul. I am the thing that goes bump in the night, and Kennedy Dover shouldn't be shackled to my evil for the rest of her life.

"So tell me! Tell me, Everett! I'm not afraid of the big, bad wolf! Give me your worst!" She's yelling, holding her arms out as if she wants me to try to attack her.

She wants the truth? She wants the Boogie Man? Fine. I'll unleash it.

"When I was taken prisoner, I didn't think there could be anything that would break me. How fucking naïve I was, and you are, too. There was this one guy, particularly specialized in acute, localized pain. Or at least that's how I thought of him in my head, I never could understand any of those fuckers. That in itself messes with you, no one speaking your language for the better part of a year, it throws you out of your element. Anyways, he used to target one specific area, one you'd never think would hurt. Or, at least you never thought about being hurt in that place. Take the eardrums, for explain. There was this one week he'd pop one of my eardrums every day. Do you know how much that shit hurts? It also steals your balance, so I'd barely be able to stand, or prepare for when they came into my cell to beat me. He'd rip off fingernails, send electroshocks through my nose, one time he used a drill to—"

"*Stop* it. Stop it!" Kennedy's voice is a broken thing as she places a hand on my arm.

I flinch. "I told you not to touch me."

"I'm sorry. It's just ... I understand. I guess I don't, because how could I? What you went through sounds like hell. But, you lived. You came out on the other side. You must have found something deep within you while they had you that helped you push through."

It's at this moment that I realize she still thinks there is a positive that came from my entrapment. That the ending is one of a hero, some brave blockbuster movie finish with redemption and rescue.

That's why she, and everyone else, will never understand. I didn't pull myself through with thoughts of home. I didn't visualize her face, or strengthen my mind with fantasies of a normal life.

There is just a point, after you cross into a certain pain threshold, after every hope and flicker of positivity is stolen from you, that you just go numb. My body was on autopilot after a time, not allowing me to live but not allowing me to die either. I'm not back here because I want to be, because I saved my own life by perseverance.

If it was all the same to me, I'd rather they offed me in that goddamn filthy bunker. It would be better than living like this. There are just certain people, after they experience the level of trauma I have, who should be put out of their misery. Like a sick dog, someone should just put us down.

And then Kennedy says the last words I ever expect to hear.

"I know what it's like to watch someone die."

21

"I know what it's like to watch someone die." My tone is hushed, and Everett's head snaps up.

His eyes are a hard, flinty clover, as if the green is seeping out of him the more furious he grows. "You have no idea what you're talking about."

When I got off of my night shift, I thought I'd be scurrying to my car in the cold. Not bumping into the next Michael Myers, who happens to be my next door neighbor, shredding his own hero banner.

Before I said anything, I watched Everett go to town on the plastic sign, knifing it with such anger that it stole my breath. His rage, it was palpable through the air, and even though I'm furious at him for what happened at the diner, I couldn't let him self-destruct like that. Maybe I hadn't realized, up until this point, just what he'd been through.

Hearing him describe his torture makes me physically ill, and I still feel like I could bend over and empty the contents of my stomach on my shoes.

But I need to tell him this, to tell him that I know a fraction of what he went through.

"Maybe I don't. I can't begin to understand what you went through, the horrible things you've seen. But I've seen horrible things too. I've held someone's hand as they took their last breath. I've watched a man struggle through a heart attack, only to lose the battle. I've seen a family thrown from their vehicle, all four of them including their children—"

I break off, not able to complete my sentence because of the sob making its way out of my throat.

Everett assesses me, skeptical and guarded but with a shimmer of understanding passing over his face.

Swiping at the tears I can't keep from falling down my cheeks, I speak directly to him. "The point is, I know what death looks like. I know firsthand how horrible it can be to deal with that. And if you want to talk about what you went through, I'm here. No matter what's gone on between us, I'm here. But don't think that just because you did some terrible things for the greater good of your country ... don't think it still doesn't make you a hero. You dared to do things not a lot of people could stomach. That alone should mean something."

His eyes change, and it's the tiniest shift in the energy between us, but I feel it.

I know it's going to happen before he makes a move. This moment, the one I've been imagining and wishing for since I first knew the word crush, it's about to come true.

Everett steps into me, sweat trickling down his brow, and my heart vibrates so hard in my chest, I think it might just pop out. The kiss at the diner is all but forgotten. This is the moment we were meant to have, the slow, pulse-pounding first touch that the universe fated for us.

His hand comes up to my cheek, and my eyes flutter closed, then open slowly. I want to shut them, but I also want to see his face until the very last second. Those green eyes are full of lust, but also concern and restraint. Is he as afraid as I am?

Inside, I'm freaking out. My heart is going a mile a minute, and the hand that just wrapped itself around the back of Everett's neck is shaking. I press up on my toes, ready to meet his mouth as it descends to mine.

For the briefest of moments, our lips only touch. That point of contact, the only one I'll ever remembering existing between me and another human after this, is so *right* and *pure* I want to cry. We don't move, neither of us seeks for more, we just taste and breathe and remain still.

Then Everett breaks, and the floodgates open. His hands dive into my hair, my fingers grip the nape of his neck and pull at the collar of his sweatshirt to bring him as close as possible. Our lips punish each other, working in a rhythm I am sure I'll never find with anyone else.

When his tongue slips inside my mouth, I groan at the same time a husky growl vibrates from Everett's throat. We're alone on the dark town square, this carnal session of kissing for our eyes only. It's been such a long time coming, that neither of us seem to be able to control ourselves. We're trying for too much, too fast, but then again, how else was this supposed to go?

"*Perfect*. You are perfect." He breathes onto my lips.

It's only a split second that Everett pulls back, but in no time, we're seeking each other out, our mouths clawing to get back to one another.

And as we continue this torrid make-out session, born of passion and anger and fate, I know it for a fact now.

Everett Brock has ruined me for any other man.

If he doesn't want me after this, I'm not sure how I'll survive.

22

"Did he text you yet?"

The question Bianca has been asking me every morning at our breakfast table in the cafeteria grates on my nerves.

"Not yet, Bi. When he does, you'll be the first to know," I mumble, picking at my chocolate chip muffin but having zero appetite.

Everett kissed me on the street at midnight and hasn't been in touch since. When I got home that night, I laid awake in bed, wondering if he was doing the same thing while thinking about me. That kiss, it's the one I've been waiting for my entire life. I thought once it happened, once we finally reached that point, that all the other issues would work themselves out.

Clearly, since it's been exactly a week since Everett has spoken to me or even bothered coming around, that's not the case.

"He's an asshole. I can't believe it. No, actually I can. Everett Brock has always had that fuckboy vibe to him." Rachel nods at her own opinion.

I shrug, not wanting to talk about this at all. Not only do I have a huge trigonometry test today, but I have my college acceptances to worry about for the next five months, so I have plenty to stress about.

"Do you want to go to Everdeen this weekend?" Bianca changes the subject.

Rach claps her hands. "Oh my God, yes! Graden texted Scott the other day and they're throwing this huge rager at their house off campus."

Everdeen is the university about an hour from Brentwick, and it's one that a lot of the students from our high school attend. Some would call it Brentwick 2.0, but I just call it too close to home. I didn't even apply, because I know there would be too many familiar faces. I want a challenge, somewhere that I can forge my own path and meet new types of people.

Rach and Bi, and the group of our friends that often accompany on weekend adventures, always want to go to Everdeen. It's a guaranteed party, with guaranteed alcohol, and is just far enough out of parent supervision that there is little risk of punishment. I've gone a couple times, and it's always fun. But, I'm just not into it this week.

"Count me out. I just don't feel up to it right now, girls, I'm sorry."

I know I'm being a bummer, but it's all just caught up to me. My best friends exchange a worried look, but they keep their mouths shut.

If only I had an answer, then I wouldn't feel such turmoil rolling around my gut. I'm stuck in limbo, waiting to see if that perfect kiss was just a one-time thing, or if Everett is ready for the possibility of more between us. I'm pathetic, I know this, but when you wait years for a guy, it's pretty hard to just cut off all feelings.

Severing the part of me that's in love with Everett Brock has never worked, no matter how hard I've tried. Even when I thought he was gone from this world, my heart ached to be with him. Now that he's kissed me, that I've tasted what it's like to experience that, it's going to take a lot of strength to move on from it if he rejects me.

"Hey." Logan sidles up next to me, his big form taking over the table.

"Hey." I give him a small smile.

He has no idea what's been going on with Everett, though he has been texting me to ask if I'm planning to go here or there during the weekend, and how my days have been. I know that Logan is trying to start something, and he's a nice guy, but as has already been demonstrated, I don't feel an ounce for him what I do for Everett.

"How's your week?" he asks, unwrapping a bacon, egg, and cheese biscuit from the local deli that he must have picked up before school.

I shrug. "It's okay, busy with some tests. How about you?"

"Just peachy." He grins through a bite. "But we have to stay late at practice tonight, have some extra drills today or some shit. Everett is the assistant coach running our unit now, and he's a total dick. The guy hates me. Clearly." Logan throws me a side-eye.

My cheeks heat up, and I know they must be at least pink. "About that ... that wasn't supposed to happen. I was really caught off guard. It was rude for it to happen in front of you."

We haven't talked about what Everett did at the diner, and he also has no idea that Everett kissed me again on the street.

Logan just gives me a good-natured shrug. "People have histories, I get that. It seems complicated, and not so fun. Me? I'm fun. I won't put too much pressure on you, and I think you're pretty damn special, Kennedy. So, if you want to keep hanging out, I'll be here."

I am a real idiot. Here is a handsome, kind guy who gets

along with my friends and doesn't have any demons hiding in his closet, for all I know. I should say yes, that I want to hang out with him. In my final months before leaving Brentwick, I should be looking for a fun, maybe sexy time with someone who won't grow attached.

Even though all of that might be true, my heart isn't interested in logic.

It's invested in Everett Brock, rational thought be damned.

23

I'm not sure what lures me to the woods behind my house, but my restless brain won't sleep and this has always been the solution.

After they came to tell us that Everett was presumed dead, I spent many nights out in the trees, walking the familiar path to the tree house that the owner's long before my parents had built for their children. It was a hideout, a sanctuary, and in our later years, Rachel, Bianca and I would sneak out to meet here if one of us was going through something. And since they're at Everdeen without me this weekend, on account of my total lack of excitement to step foot there, I need a hideout of my own.

Technically, it's not anywhere close to my backyard. My parents barely remember that it's here, it's so far into the forest. If they knew I was traipsing almost half a mile into the wooded area behind our house, they'd be seriously pissed off.

I'm no longer afraid, though, as the tree house and the woods around it have kind of become my place of solace. Just like Batman has his Bat Cave, and Superman has his Fortress of Solitude, Kennedy Dover has her shabby tree house in the suburban Jersey forest. It's nothing fancy, though I've kept a blanket and some pillows and a flashlight up there since I began making frequent night visit, but it's mine. In every aspect of my life, I'm expected to be *on*. Vivacious, intelligent, focused. I'm the girl everyone expects to have a plan or a goal in everything I do. Out here, I can let it all go. Sometimes I cry. Sometimes I let myself dare to dream about leaving it all behind, going on the road and never looking back. I don't have to answer to anyone in the tree house, least of all, myself.

When I reach the large oak that houses the fourteen-by-ten wood structure high in its branches, only the sounds of crickets keep me company. I'm about to ascend the ladder, feeling for the familiar hunks of wood nailed into the tree. I've climbed this dozens of times in the dark, and even more in the light.

A hand snakes around my upper arm just as I reach for the first plank and wrenches me back.

"Oh my God!" I scream, fear slamming into me like a tractor trailer.

The figure clamps its hand down on my mouth, pulling me into it. My heart hammers against my ribcage, and I literally see my life flash before my eyes. This is it, I'm going to die. My body will be left out here, all because I couldn't sleep and felt too secure in my suburban town.

The fight-or-flight instinct in me both kick in as I realize I need to escape. Wriggling, I struggle against the body, but it's too overpowering. I might be scrappy, and against another person I'd have good odds, but this mysterious lurker is far too strong. I can barely move an inch, that's how tight of a hold *it* has on me.

"Stop fighting me. Be quiet," the voice commands in my ear.

Instantly, the blood drains from my face; I feel it, but my relieved breath whooshes out onto the palm blocking my mouth. In one second, I'm both calmed and terrified.

Because I'm not here alone. I'm not going to be left for dead. No, I'm here with Everett.

"What are you doing out here?" My voice cracks on the question, and I sound half insane.

"Trying not to be convicted of assault on a teenage girl, if you'd keep your voice down," he clips out, but doesn't release me.

I'm acutely aware, at this moment, of our proximity to each other. My back is pressed to his front, all the muscles he now sports rigid against my limbs as they hold me. His hand covers my mouth, but at an odd angle, so that the tips of his fingers caress the corner of my lips. At first, I'm not sure he realizes he's stroking his thumb against my bottom one.

Involuntarily, my back arches at the tiny gesture of exploration, my butt pressing into his groin. An electrical charge ignites between us, whipping through the air and pebbling goose bumps up my skin. I wore a sweater and Ugg boots out here, aware of the chill, but now I'm burning under the restricting clothing.

Everett's breath is husky in my ear, my vision still straight ahead at the tree, with the fort lingering above us.

"What are *you* doing out here?" he accuses, not letting go.

I stay stock still. "This is my backyard, so I shouldn't have to answer that. But, if you must know, I come out here when I can't sleep."

"Seems like an awfully dangerous thing to do. Any murderer or creep could be waiting to pounce."

"Are you calling yourself a murderer? Or just a creep?" I throw back, annoyed at how turned-on I am.

He's been nothing but callous and awful since he got home, something I've tried to dismiss. But now he's messing with my alone time, at *my* tree house, and I'm tired of the antics. Plus, he hasn't bothered to call or see me since we rocked the shit out of each other's worlds with that kiss, so I'm extra pissed.

"I've killed people in cold blood, shot them right in the head.

I guess that makes me a murderer." His voice takes on an odd note I can't place.

That should chill my blood, but it only makes my heart weep. What's become of the boy next door?

"Up you go." He flourishes a hand, those pearly whites sneaking out as he smirks. Or maybe it's a snarl.

All I know is, his smile hasn't looked the same since he came home.

I should tell him to leave me alone, to go back to his house. Part of me protests the idea of getting into an enclosed space with him. It seems like we've been simmering for a while now, and if push comes to shove, we'll boil over. I'm not sure I want to know what happens then.

Especially after the last time. We had the most perfect of first —well, okay, technically second—kisses, and he's now looking at me like I'm dirt again.

At the same time, though, I'd be a damn liar if I wasn't jittery with excitement at the prospect of being close to him. Goddamn my foolish heart.

"Why are you out here?" I say as I crest the landing, pulling myself up onto the weathered floorboards.

"I guess I'm looking for the same thing you are." Everett pulls himself up behind me and looks out at the dark forest.

"I don't want to play games anymore," I whisper, because my heart can't take this. "Either we ... do this. Or we don't."

He turns, life dancing in his eyes. Sparks of energy light as he stalks toward me.

"I don't want to play. I don't want to *not* play. But I can't help it."

Before I can argue with him, tell him to stop fucking with my mind and heart, Everett crushes his lips to mine. And I know what I just said, what I've felt for the week he hasn't called or bothered to explain the kiss in town square.

But this is *us* we're talking about. Something I've wanted for so long. And while we're out here in the dark, my shame and rejection can take a back seat if no one is here to witness it.

Everett engulfs me, walking me backward as he kisses me until my back collides with the rough wood wall of the tree house. My tongue invades his mouth, the kiss deepening to a passionate, crazed level that I know won't stop like the one in town square.

I pull his sweatshirt up and over his head, the sound of Everett hissing through his teeth as I graze his naked flesh hitting my ears like the best kind of music. It's dark, the tree house barely letting any moonlight in, and I can hardly see a thing. But my fingers rove, hitting muscles after muscle, feeling his skin in a way I've only dreamed about.

When I get to his back, that's when I feel them. The divots, the raised scars, the long, jagged sections that I'm sure stand out in the daylight. I've tried to put this part of his homecoming to the back of my mind, where I don't have to address it. But I saw it the other night in town square, and I'm feeling it now.

The boy next door was tortured, maybe to within an inch of his life, and it's no wonder he can't open up to anyone. I want to hold him, just cradle him in my arms.

Just then, Everett's lips and stubble work their way down my cheek, to my jaw, nipping and kissing a path to this spot behind my earlobe that—

"Oh my God!" I all but shriek.

The sensation he just elicited is one I've never felt before, and it hits me square between the thighs.

"You taste like fucking heaven," he growls, doing something sinful to my body that reduces it to a puddle.

But I can't fully give in.

"You didn't call." I breathe, my head spinning with his lips on my neck.

Everett pulls back, his green eyes blazing as he drinks me in. "I can't think straight when it comes to you."

Before I can say another word, his lips are back on mine, and those large hands are flirting with the hem of my sweater. Arching into him, until I can't get any closer, I give him silent permission to take it off. Before he pulls back to remove it, I'm pressed against the large, rigid form of his arousal, so clear and present between us.

It's big, and I know I have no experience, but I wonder idly just how that would fit inside me.

Slowly, so slowly that I want to scream at him to tear it off, Everett lifts my sweater from my torso, then over my head. We press together, our bare upper-halves, in the freezing cold.

But I'm so, *so* hot. Burning up against him, as he curses under his breath and fills his palms with my bra cups.

"You're so goddamn beautiful," he bites it out like it pains him.

All I can do is blink, he's reduced me to a mindless, needy thing. I press up, kissing him as our arms twine around each other. With each lap of a tongue, nibble of a lip, I'm brought closer to the brink of something I can't quite describe.

As if he knows the cure, Everett stops us, grabbing his sweat-shirt and laying it on the wooden plank floor. Then he maneuvers me until I'm lying down, the muscles of his bicep bulging as he lies on his side hovering above me.

"Do you trust me?" A lock of golden hair flops onto his forehead, making him look even more devastatingly gorgeous.

I should say no. I should say that he's been sending me up and down like a roller coaster for weeks. But I don't. Because I do trust him.

Gulping, I nod. I can't possibly speak right now.

His hand crosses the boundary of the waistline of my black leggings, moving down as my heart thunders in my chest. I squirm, so turned-on that I can feel the wetness coating my thighs and between my legs. I should be embarrassed, or self-conscious, but all I feel right now is an arousal so sharp, I need relief.

Everett looks like he's in agony, his head dropping to my chest, brushing kisses up and down my cleavage.

When he finally reaches my center, one finger sliding up and down my crease, I almost explode. My hips buck as electric shocks vibrate through my body. Everett brings his mouth back to mine, kissing me until I see stars. As I squirm against his hand, I don't realize he pushes a finger into me until a sharp pain makes me cry out into his mouth.

"It's okay, give it a minute." He stills every part of his body.

The pain consumes me for a minute, until it starts to fade, the edges fizzling into pleasure. I seek his lips, trying to tell him it's okay to keep going. He takes the hint, stroking inside me. *My God*, is this why everyone chases these encounters? I feel so *good*, so free.

Everett moves his finger faster, plunging into me as he kisses me senseless. When he adds another finger, something happens. It's as if a trigger is pulled, something inside me snaps and fires.

I can't catch my breath, my limbs won't stop shaking, I might be crying or cursing but I can't hear a sound my mind is so gone. Everett is chanting my name, telling me to let it all go. I follow the feeling, ride the high of it, until my vision begins to come back.

Holy crap. So, *that's* an orgasm.

As I come down, I realize the milestone I've just crossed. I'm no longer a girl, one who wonders about sex and experiences and men. I've joined the club, the one where things become all that more dangerous but all that more fun.

Reaching for Everett's pants, which are now tented to the

point that I can see down them and the obvious bulge peeking out of his waistband, my mouth goes dry. I want to do this; I want it to be good for him, but I have no idea what I'm doing.

He puts his hand over mine. "Kennedy. This was about you. I've dreamed about seeing you like that for ... Christ, for a long time. Tonight was about you."

His words are more gentle and compassionate than I've heard from him in the entirety of his return to Brentwick. Here I am, thinking a monster is slowly pulling my heart into the darkness, along with his own, when he decides to surprise me.

Twisted, lonely Everett is one I can almost hate, one I can guard myself against.

But I have absolutely no chance against the boy who just gave me an unselfish gift. I have no shot if he starts speaking to me, treating me in the tender way he is now.

And I don't want one.

24

Another muscle pops somewhere in my jaw, and I know that if I continue to grind my teeth during this game, I'll lose a molar.

But goddammit, he's looking at her like she's a piece of meat and his next meal is a juicy, center cut steak.

"MYERS!" I explode. "Get your fucking helmet on, you're going in."

No mind that he's not a very good player and we're down by two touchdowns, but if he doesn't get his eyes off of Kennedy, I'm going to fucking uppercut him.

It's been a week since I made her come in the tree house, and I haven't been able to stop thinking about it since. The way she looked as she unraveled, the endless amount of time we spent kissing, how I freely got to touch her after so many years of trying not to.

Fuck, it was heaven. And not something I'm sure I can repeat. Because what happens if I let her in, and she truly sees my soul. What happens when I hurt her, which is inevitable, what then? Kennedy has always been the girl I wanted to end up with. And if it ends, what will I have left?

It's why I haven't seen her. Why I haven't texted. I'm sure it looks like I'm an asshole, hell I *am* an asshole. But it doesn't mean I'm going to stand here while Logan Myers makes fuck-me eyes at her and she smiles back.

One of our coach's calls a timeout, and I stalk over to where she stands on the sidelines, in formation with the other cheerleaders.

I want to grab her arm, drag her to my car and kiss the hell out of her, but that would look pretty bad to this crowd. Plus, my knifed-up hero banner was discovered in the town square, and people have been asking questions. I don't need more attention thrown my way.

"Can we talk?" I bite out, standing close to her.

She keeps up her peppy smile, but I see the panic in her big brown eyes. "Not right now, I'm cheering."

"I don't care." My voice is all restraint.

"Everett—"

"This is not a request. Come with me now, or I'll put you over my shoulder again."

An audible sigh leaves her lips, and she turns to talk to Rachel for a brief moment before shrugging at me and motioning to lead the way.

Without an explanation to my other coaches, my position is purely for show anyway so who cares if I disappear in the middle of a game, I make my way around the bleachers. You'd think there would be people making out down here, or doing drugs. Typical high school shit. But all that's there to witness our conversation is some old football practice pads and a couple empty Gatorade coolers.

And once we're back here, alone, I get all up in her space.

"If he doesn't stop looking at you, I'm going to rip out his throat," I snarl, so close to her lips that I can taste the cherry seltzer she was drinking.

Kennedy rolls her eyes so hard, I fear they might not sit right in their sockets afterward. "Cut the shit. Logan and I are friends. And last time I checked, I can smile at whoever I want."

My fists shake at my sides. "You don't want to test me on this, Kennedy."

Before I know what's happening, she shoves me. *Hard*. Anger radiates from her body, and I know I've hit a nerve.

"You don't want me. You've never truly wanted me. You talk a big game and let your ego do the walking, but when it really comes down to it, you never commit. For years, I was right there for the taking. I would have been yours in a second if you just snapped your fingers. Hell, I'd have even fallen at your feet when you came home just months ago. But you don't really want that, do you, Everett? Attention. Validation. That's what you want. This is more about your bruised soul than it is about wanting to be with me. And that's just vicious to me, Everett."

Her tone isn't cutting, it isn't mean or rude. It's ... resigned. Which may be even worse. I've jerked her around so much, to the point where Kennedy doesn't even think I have feelings for her.

If she only knew how fucking much I want her, how much I lust over her, how much I want to make her mine. But I just can't tell her.

I know I'm sending mixed signals, but it's only because my own brain is so damn disheveled from everything I've been through. Deep down, I know it will never be possible for me to love Kennedy the way she needs. I'm too damaged, the things I need to overcome would sink us in the end.

But every so often, when I'm reminded that she will leave me behind for someone else, a surge of carelessness washes over me. I don't give a damn about the consequences, that I shouldn't go after her. I just want her. And so I do something fucking stupid, like kissing her in that diner, or pulling her aside right now.

"That's not true. None of that is true." My heart aches to tell her the truth.

"Whatever. I can't do this anymore." Her tone has a note of finality, and I panic.

"Get in the car." I toss my chin in the direction of the parking lot. "I want to take you somewhere."

I command her, but she doesn't move.

"And why would I get in any car with you? You haven't driven in over two years. Plus, it's the middle of the game."

That's not true, but she doesn't know that. It's been about three weeks since my parents let me start using the car again, and only after I told them I picked some community college courses. It's how I've been avoiding Kennedy so well. I've been driving myself to other towns, to the outskirts of Brentwick, anywhere I don't have to have run-ins with her.

"Who cares? Please, give me one last chance."

It's now or never. She just laid her cards out, revealed to me exactly what I've been showing her, how I've been treating her. And now it's time for the Hail Mary play, because I've fucked this up so bad, I'm going to lose her.

I didn't realize until this moment just how much I can't let that happen.

So I have to tell her. All of it.

25

Driving through a graveyard at dusk is, as assumed, creepy.

The headstones start to cast long shadows, massive portions of the land are bathed in darkness, while the sun plays tricks with your eyes in others. It's quiet, and when you're the only car weaving its way through the narrow passages, the feeling of isolation is real.

I pull the car to a stop at the space my mom directed me to last week, when she first brought me here. I'd asked her to, a day after my encounter with Kennedy in the tree house. I'd felt the most normal, the most like myself, after I was with her in the most intimate way possible. I was ready to face my fears, to see the worst of what could have happened.

When I look over at Kennedy, she looks like she isn't breathing. Her eyes are wide, and I think I might have really scared her. This is probably the last place she thought I'd bring her.

Laying a hand over hers, I say gently, "Come on, please?"

She unbuckles herself and follows as I get out too, walking up the grassy hill to the spot where I need us both to stand at.

"So, this is where they buried me." I survey the headstone as if it actually reads my cause of death.

"I know. I was there." Kennedy breathes beside me, and I notice her shivering.

Shit, it's practically Thanksgiving, and it's frigid out here. Without being invited, I wrap an arm around her shoulder, tucking her into me. Her eyes flutter up to me, and I can almost see her here on that day.

"Did you cry?" I ask, curious.

"Of course I did." She says this as if it's obvious.

"Sometimes, I wonder if anyone back home cared about me, when I was down in that hole." It rolls off my tongue without me even thinking about it.

And even though she's still snuggled into me, I hear Kennedy sigh.

"Can we put a stop to this now? This back and forth. I don't want to be a pawn in your game. It hurts, Everett. You know how I feel about you. And don't lie and tell me you don't feel the same way, too."

I look down at her, pushing a lock of hair off her face. "I'm sorry. I'm not trying to hurt you. Or maybe I was. Because I was so hurt. But, I'm ready to tell you why. Will you listen?"

As we stand there, in front of my grave, I give Kennedy the most vulnerable side of me. I just hope she accepts it.

"Yes." She looks so deep into my soul that I'm almost tempted to shut back up again.

But I know this is the only way to get her to trust me, to possibly get her to be with me.

"When I first signed up for the military, I was so cocky. I thought I was a big shot, some noble countryman who was going to blow some enemies' heads off. That couldn't be further from the truth. I was so in over my head from day one, it wasn't even funny. I hadn't considered that there were actual lives at the end of my scope, that I was killing people with families and interests and *breath*. I was good at it, don't get me wrong. It's why they recruited me for black ops missions, which I thought made me even bigger than I thought I was. But it steals a part of you, every life you take. I wasn't prepared for that. It leaves this gaping hole inside you, that just keeps rotting away. And then I was asked to do this thing. An unimaginable thing. I can't tell you about it, believe me you wouldn't look at me the same ever again if you knew what it was. But I didn't go through with it, and that's how I ended up getting captured."

Chancing a look at Kennedy, her eyes are trained on my face, tears glistening.

Gulping, I continue. "When I was imprisoned ... it was fucking terrible. But worse than that, there are just no words to describe. I'm sure everyone around here has their theories about how I was treated, and maybe you can imagine the worst. I'm telling you, it was a thousand times more horrific than what you picture in your nightmares. And not just the physical torture, although pain is just a word when you're that deep in agony that you barely feel anymore. No, the mental fuck-all they put me through was worse. Threatening my family, my fellow soldiers. Speaking in tongues in front of me, blasting music, not allowing me to sleep. I wished I would die, so I didn't have to go through it anymore. I'm not sure you, or anyone else, will ever grasp what it feels like to be there, to feel like you'd actually rather die than keep on living in conditions like that. So ... that's why I'm so fucked up. It's why I can't give you a straight answer, or why I disappear after being vulnerable with you. Believe me, Kennedy, I wish I wasn't like this. I'd give anything to be the guy from those letters, because I meant every word. I'm just not sure I can give those things to you anymore."

Kennedy sighs, and we stare at my grave, the silence deafening. My arms still hold her, but I can feel the distance growing.

I've told her as much as I can tell her, bared my soul so that she might understand. Will it be enough?

"When they told me you had died, that you were gone, I wanted to curl up into the earth myself. We had just spent a whole year writing to each other, about everything we wished we could be. The things you wrote to me, they were what I'd always dreamed you'd say. If I had to live in a world where you no longer existed, I wasn't sure I would be able to do that. Everett, I imagined so many things. I imagined a future where you came home for me."

Her words slice my heart open and seem to empty all the poison I've been holding onto for months.

"And then you came home, and you weren't *you*. You weren't the man from those letters, or the one I'd imagined being with. Do you know how hurtful you've been over the last few months?"

Turning to her, pulling her in so that were flush against each other, I try to stare every amount of emotion I feel straight into her chocolate brown eyes.

"I'm sorry. I'm so sorry, Kennedy. Some days, I can't tell which way is up. Don't you get it? I don't think I deserve to be here. One day, the enemy all just up and left. I have no idea why they didn't just *off me* before they went. Maybe they were in a rush. Maybe they figured I was already on my way to death, the desert would finish me off. With every step I took, every look over my shoulder, I was sure someone was fucking with me. That I'd get a bullet to the back, or some fucking militia fighter would jump out and slit my throat. I still feel like that. Why the fuck am I here, how did I make it home? It doesn't seem real still. To have you so happy to see me home, to have you still be the same incredible, gorgeous woman you were when I left—I can't grapple with it sometimes. I don't deserve you. I'm too tainted, too destroyed."

"And yet, I still want you." She shrugs, as if we're stuck in this impossible situation.

"I've never wanted anything as much as I want you." I breathe, relief flooding through me.

I've waited so long to say those words to her in person, and I'm finally releasing myself to do so. I'm tired of fighting it, of trying to predict the future of when I'll hurt her. My life is fucked up enough already, I'm done with trying to close myself off. If I don't open up, I'm going to end up in that grave for real, buried beneath the earth. Dr. Liu has told me as much, and Kennedy just laid it on me.

"I don't want you looking at Logan Myers, or him looking at you. I want you. I want you to be with me. You're ... *Christ*, Kennedy, you're so damn perfect it's intimidating."

Her long dark locks shake with her head. "I'm not. I have so many flaws, Everett, and a lot of them have to do with wanting you even when you push me away. But, I guess that's how we got here, huh?"

I just thank the heavens that she doesn't take no as an answer very easily. For all the shit I've thrown her way, before and after returning to Brentwick, she should have kicked my ass to the curb long ago. I have a lot of making up to do. And I plan to start now.

My fingers trace her jaw. "No more games. Let's do this. I can't promise I won't be surly, or closed off, but I want to try."

Kennedy blinks up at me. "I've been waiting a long time to hear you say that."

"So, say yes." I breathe, bending until my whisper fans over her lips.

"Ye—"

She can't get the full syllable out. I don't let her.

Because when my mouth covers hers, in the first time as two

people who have pledged their hearts to one another, it isn't patient.

There, over the shadow of my gravestone, I give her the kiss I've been waiting a decade to give her. And it feels all that much more real because she is finally mine.

26

KENNEDY

Two weeks pass before the night of the big barn party on Thanksgiving Eve.

They're filled with hours of schoolwork, goofing off with Rachel and Bi, EMT shifts, and worrying about my college acceptance letters. Oh, and of course, fitting in every spare second I can with Everett.

Since the night at his headstone, where we agreed to no more games, he's been ... *incredible*. Everything I envisioned a relationship with Everett would look like, is what we have had these past two weeks. Texting and talking all hours of the day. Sneaking glances at each other across the football field. Hanging out with my friends on weekend nights. He came over for dinner with my parents.

And best of all, we sneak out of our houses most nights to spend them with each other in the tree house. While there has been no sex, or talk of it, we've come pretty damn close. I gave my first hand job, and then blow job, this past week. I don't think I was particularly great, but Everett made it sound like I was and I got the desired end result, so I couldn't have been *that* bad.

But tonight, you'd think all of that had never happened.

Thanksgiving Eve is the biggest night of drinking, well, prob-ably everywhere in the United States. Everyone comes home from college, or from out of town if they've graduated. Exes meet up, hook up, old friends drift back into town in search of their mom's turkey and end up doing shots of tequila with the kid they sat next to in ninth grade Spanish. It's tradition for everyone to venture out to the barn where parties are held, and spend the last hours before sitting down at a table with your family getting absolutely plastered.

So here we are, sitting on Scott's tailgate that's parked in front of the enormous bonfire, surrounded by hundreds of people. There are kids six years older than I am here, hitting on the juniors who got invited to this party, which is kind of disgusting, but far be it from me to cock block. Some of my previous cheer captains showed up, and we all played flip cup together. Bianca's ex-boyfriend is lurking, and Rachel has already threatened to knee him in the family jewels.

But it's Everett I can't keep my eyes off of. Most of his old high school buddies came home for the holiday, and he's turned into the senior I lusted after once again. I've seen a smile on his face more than once, and I swear he even laughed.

Though the reason I may or may not be on my third cran-berry and vodka is because he hasn't bothered treating me like his ... well, girlfriend. Are we boyfriend and girlfriend? He asked me to be together with him, but we never made it official with titles. Do we need them? Isn't our connection deeper than that?

Well, maybe not. My friends know about us and have hung out with us. But do his? Everett hasn't brought me over to his house, so maybe his parents don't even know.

All of my insecurities as a teenage girl, especially one who has been so tossed around by her love interest, creep out and invade my blood like poison.

I've just been openly staring at him throughout the night,

willing him to look at me, but he hasn't. Hasn't come up to kiss me, or put his arm around me, or introduce me to his friends. Of course, they all know me, just not as *his* girl. How badly I want to be called *his girl.*

"Why are those guys running through the fire?" Bianca yelps.

"Because men are idiots who want to measure their dick size without whipping it out?" Rachel poses this as a question, but it's more of a statement.

"Truth." I giggle, rolling my eyes as I tip my mixed drink up.

The tart liquid slides down my throat, and I momentarily don't care that the guy I'm practically getting naked with is ignoring me.

"Come on, soldier, show me those muscles!" Trent, one of the guys who ran in the same circle as Everett in high school, whips off his flannel, revealing a slate of abs.

Something low in my stomach begins to buzz, an electric current of butterflies zapping my core. Everett has a twinkle in his eye, the glint of the fire glistening off of his third, or maybe fourth, beer. He's been happy tonight, in the company of his friends, and seems relaxed. In that regard, I can't be salty about tonight. I love seeing him happy.

"You call those abs? More like a dad bod," he quips, elbowing another buddy as they laugh at Trent.

"My point exactly, they can't stop this pissing contest if they tried." Rachel points to where the boys stand across the fire.

"Don't worry, baby, I know my body is the best out of all of these assholes." Scott quirks an eyebrow at her.

Rachel snorts. "Keep your shirt on, hun."

Before I know what's happening, Everett is whipping his sweater over his head, the soft cream-colored garment dropping down onto the dirt.

"Holy shit," Bianca deadpans, openly staring at the guy I've been crushing on since I can remember.

My jaw drops open, because *goddamn*, it's impossible not to stare. It's been pitch-black in the tree house, so I can never truly see what my fingers are running over. Now that it's on full display, in front of all of these people at the barn, I'm frozen.

Stunned.

Everett is ... wow. I thought he was hot before, when I used to see him after football practice or in his backyard mowing the lawn with his shirt off. But this? He has the body of a man. Abs carved of steel. Arms that could hold back hundreds of enemy forces. A waist that was both agile and firm, with a—

"Do you see that penis ravine? Jesus Christ." Rachel reads my thoughts.

Bianca chokes on a laugh. "Oh my God, penis ravine is right. You could pour liquid danger down those things."

My cheeks burst into flames. "Guys, seriously? That's gross."

Actually, the name is hilarious, but Everett has swung his gaze our way and I know he just heard Rachel's little nicknames for the muscles leading right to his, well ...

Penis.

"Um, no it's not. That's a beautiful sight right there." Bianca bows as if Everett's abs are royalty.

And while I can't help but stare, and my loins are ablaze with the need to touch said royal abs, I'm pissed. He hasn't bothered to even come check on me tonight, much less act like we're together, which we said we are. And now he's taking off his clothes for a hundred people we went to high school with? Clearly, attention isn't something he's trying to shy away from.

It's just attention with *me* he's shying away from.

A flip switches in me, and probably the three vodka cranberries that aid it. I don't need him to come over to me. I'm not this desperate, needy girl. I won't wait around for the guy I'm with to acknowledge me. If I want him, I'm going to get him.

Marching across the party without another word, it takes about twenty clomps of my boots in the dust to reach Everett. Once I do, I'm pushing him backward, like a force not to be reckoned with, as his astonished face sparkles down at me. My fingers tangle in the ridiculously sexy hair on his chest, and an expression of amusement plays on his good looks as he doesn't resist, but moves backward as I push him.

I hear the catcalls in the distance, the wolf whistles of our mutual friends. But I don't stop until we're well out into the woods, probably in the same spot Everett dragged me to that time over his shoulder.

"Well, if you wanted me, I guess I know the way to get your attention now." He winks, grazing his nails up and down his abs once I stop and drop my hand.

Momentarily distracted by his own preening of himself, which makes me clench my thighs, I forget my train of thought.

And then it's back. "Wait, what? To get me to notice you? You're the one who has been ignoring me the whole night!" *Way to not sound desperate or needy, Kennedy.*

Everett looks surprised and reaches out a hand to cup my chin. "I was keeping my distance. Thought you'd want a fun night with your friends. And I admit I was having too much guy fun time with my own. But God, have I wanted to come over and lick that cranberry juice off your lips."

Oh. *Shit.* I'd spent so many years afraid to approach Everett, and in recent months gone out of my way not to be screamed at by him. He'd left me with many feelings of rejection, desperation, unrequited love and the sort. That now, when we've finally gotten to the root of things and were working to move forward together, I was reverting back to my old way of thinking. I guess it's only natural to think this way, since I was in it for so long.

But, I never gave Everett the benefit of the doubt that he was giving me space to have fun while he had fun, too.

"I thought, maybe, you didn't want your friends or other people to know we were ..." I trail off, not knowing what to say.

"That we're dating? That you're my girl?" Everett fills in, a knowing smile on his face. "Because you are my girl. Always have been. In case anyone was wondering."

How he says it though, it's as if he knew *I* was the one wondering. And I wasn't ready for him. Romantic Everett, I wasn't ready. I've been faced with all different types of Everett, but not this one who makes me swoon so hard I fall over.

"I like when you call me your girl." Pressing up on my toes, I lay my lips over his.

I feel the primal bristle in Everett, the way his body molds into mine. When he breaks the kiss after a few seconds, I can feel his hardness against my belly.

"Should I put you on my shoulders and parade you around the party as my girl? Will that make you feel better?"

I shake my head, laughing. "No, that'd be a bit much. But I'd like to stay here for a little while longer."

Everett smiles. "I'm yours for as long as you'll have me."

The next month goes by in a whir of activity and schedules.

The football team makes it to State, but loses. Everett was asked back for next year, though he hasn't accepted but it shows good faith in that he did a great job this season. Cheerleading ends with us coming in third place at Nationals. My EMT schedule ramps up because of my newfound freedom from cheerleading ending, as it has in years past.

And, my peers start hearing from their early decision colleges.

I didn't apply to any early decision, not wanting to get my hopes dashed too early. But I have to say, I'm green with envy of those fellow students who already have their future set. I'm left to sweat it out, crossing my fingers and praying until around March or April. This is torture, what these colleges do, but I *guess* sifting through thousands of applicants isn't a fast process.

I do have Everett through it all, though. He's been helping tamp my anxiety down with lots and lots of kissing … among other things. The way he can get my body to respond, it's like he knows it better than I do. And it's not just physical. I'll wake up to a single flower on the windshield of my car. Or walk out of school at the end of the day to him sitting on the hood of his, ready to take me for coffee or pizza. We spend weekends with my friends.

Last Saturday, he took me to New York City for the day to walk around. We visited the Bryant Park Christmas shops, ate lunch at Carmine's and saw the big Rockefeller tree all lit up before taking the train home with hot chocolate in hand. It was *perfect*.

Though, this week has been nothing but insanity. I don't know why I volunteered to help chair the Winter Wonderland dance at the high school. It's tertiary to homecoming and prom, but it's still a school dance and an excuse to flirt in pretty dresses, so everyone goes. As one of the senior girls who has a prominent role on both a sporting team and in many clubs throughout school, I'm always named when anyone wants to throw one of these events. I didn't have to say yes, but I'm a goody-goody and can't seem to stop campaigning for college even with the applications already in.

Which is how I find myself, two days before the dance, cutting out paper snowflakes in the cafeteria at nine o'clock at night.

Two other people, the senior class president and her vice president, are helping, but it's taken this long to get them all done. We still have a mountain of work to actually set up, and I'm exhausted.

"I think we should call it a night," I tell them, and they nod, agreeing with tired looks in their eyes.

By the time I get home, all I want to do is drop onto my mattress and go to sleep.

What I'm met with, though, is something I never expect.

A trail of flower petals leads to my room, and I'm about to call downstairs until I catch a glimpse of Mom ducking behind the bannister. She gives me a sly smile and a thumbs-up, so clearly she's in on whatever this is.

I haven't heard from Everett in hours, and now that I'm standing in front of my bedroom door with pink and red roses under my feet, I have a sinking suspicion I know why. Pushing it open, I reveal my room bathed in candles, and vases of roses on every surface.

"Oh my ..." I suck in a breath, marveling at the spectacle of romance before me.

In my entire short life, I've never been given flowers. None have been delivered, or left in my locker on Valentine's Day. So this? This makes me want to fall to my knees, it's so beautiful.

The path is clearly made to my window, where it stops, a note is taped to the inside.

When I get to it, I peel the note off.

K,

I have a question for you. Open the window and pick up my call.

-E

Smiling to myself, I open the window, Everett grinning from across the void. He points to the paper cup on a string, set up by a pulley-system he's rigged between our houses. Picking it up, I press it to my ear as he begins to talk.

"Remember when we did this as kids?" he asks, chuckling.

I hear his talking voice more from between the houses which are only a few feet apart rather than the paper cup, but he's being so freaking cute that I still move it to my mouth to speak.

"Yes. It didn't work then either."

Everett laughs harder. "I guess not. But I did have a question to ask you."

My heart skips a beat as I press the cup closer to my ear. I stare at him, nodding, and our eyes create what feels like a cosmic force.

"Will you go to Winter Wonderland with me?" He smiles, holding up his two crossed fingers.

As if I would say no. "Everett, did you just prompose to me?"

He chuckles. "I guess I did. But this isn't prom. Don't worry, that's coming."

My heart nearly flatlines, because if this is just for Winter Wonderland, what's he going to pull out for prom?

"Yes. I'll go to Winter Wonderland with you." I swear, my cheeks are on fire.

"Did you hear that Brentwick? Kennedy Dover is going to Winter Wonderland with me!" Everett cups his hands over his mouth and shouts.

"*Shhh*!" I whisper-screech across the void. "It's almost ten o'clock!"

"You better get to sleep then, gorgeous. Wouldn't want to miss that beauty sleep." He winks.

And although he's being sarcastic, I know the compliment is real. This feeling, this one I have with him, I would wait forever to have it. It seems like I did.

No one in the world makes me feel the way Everett Brock makes me feel.

K ennedy steals my breath.

She's kept it the entire night. From the moment she walked down the stairs of her parent's house in a form-fitting black lace dress, to the way her head laid on my chest during a slow dance.

I wanted to make Winter Wonderland everything for her that I never gave her. I didn't ask her to my proms, and I barely acknowledged her when she went to homecoming as the senior queen. It feels like destiny that we're finally here, that we finally took pictures in her living room as her mom cooed and teared up behind the camera. That I could hold her hand walking into the high school, even if I'm not a student there anymore, and grind up on her during a Top 40 song.

It also feels like fate that my parents are out tonight, staying in a neighboring town at a B and B for a friend's anniversary party. Kennedy's parents think she's staying at Rachel's house, but probably aren't fooled that she isn't right next door. I think our parents are just so happy we're finally dating, that they'll condone their children staying together while lying to their faces.

"You look incredible tonight. Not even. I don't have the words." I breathe as I back Kennedy into my bedroom.

"It feels strange to be in here for ..." She gulps, and I know she was about to say *this*.

Not that either of us have talked about *this*. I guess it's implied that if all the stars aligned and we wound up together, in a house, without parents, overnight ... that well, *something* is bound to happen.

"Relax," I tell her, trying my best to be smooth.

Inside though, I'm fucking freaking out. I've never done this either, haven't gotten this close to the sun. And she is *my sun*. The one I've waited for, the prize I've wanted to take and be claimed by. Fresh, untouched by anyone else.

When I lean in to kiss her, Kennedy bows her back, pressing her breasts into me. The soft lace of her dress indents my finger-tips as I grip her hips. Before long, our kissing turns heated, then frantic, with each of us trying to get out of our clothes.

We've done this dance plenty of times now, in the tree house, in our basements, and in my car at the barn parties. I've grown accustomed to her body, its little tics and how she responds to certain pressure and pleasure. The sounds she makes, how she practically melts when I make her come on my tongue.

Shit. If I keep fantasizing while I get Kennedy's clothes off, and with her hands where they are, I'm going to come way too quickly.

Once my chest is bare, her dress is strewn on the carpet, and our shoes are kicked off, we make out while walking our way to the bed. My hands fill with her perfect tits, searching for the nipples that I know, when rolled in between my thumb and fore-finger, will bead and make her moan.

My heart is soaring, flying somewhere above me. I think, I'm not sure, the words are on the tip of my tongue.

I'm in love with Kennedy Dover.

I've known for a while, hell, *a long time*. But as I lay her back and begin to kiss down her stomach, I'm shook that it might be the time to tell her. Am I ready for that? It took me this long to get here, to let myself be with her. And it's not without reservations every day. There are still secrets I have to keep from her, ones that if I told her I love her, would end up blowing up in my face. Would she love me back if she knew?

I shake away my thoughts, reaching to pull her underwear down her hips. But instead of her usual response of heavy breathing and moaning, or maybe saying my name, Kennedy is still on the bed.

Glancing up, I see her peering at the ceiling, muttering to herself. And my heart drops. Because I know I should have talked about this before. By not addressing it, we've put way too much pressure on the situation.

I crawl up the bed toward her, and a small smile paints my lips as I lay my body on hers, my arms circling her face.

"Whatcha doing?" I bend my neck to place a small kiss on her collarbone.

"Nothing. Sorry. I ... let's keep going. Your turn?" She is so distracted that she thinks it's time to go down on me.

"Baby, what's going on?" My tone is sincere, but gentle.

"I'm nervous, Everett. I've never done this before." She averts her eyes, staring at my arm that brackets her head.

I can read it all over her body; she's not just nervous, she's embarrassed. Rolling over to my side, so that I can face her, I palm both of her cheeks.

"Look at me." She won't focus those gorgeous brown eyes on me. "Kennedy, look at me."

She blinks up, bringing our gazes level.

"I've never done this either." I nod, convincing her before she questions me.

Kennedy gasps. "You haven't? I thought for sure—"

"I've been waiting for you," I tell her, because it's the truth.

Her expression is priceless. Clearly, she did not think this was even a possibility. That we were both virgins. That we would lose it to each other.

"I couldn't take your first kiss. But I can be your first. And it doesn't have to be tonight. I've waited a long time to be with you, Kennedy. It took me a while, and I'm stubborn as hell, but I've always known it's you. If I have to wait a little longer, then I'm okay with that."

"I don't think I'm ready yet." I see tears in her eyes.

"Baby, don't cry. I'm happy just to lie here and fall asleep next to you." I brush them away from her bottom lashes.

And I mean it. This is so big of a moment, and when I finally do sink into her, when we become the most intimate two people can be, I want her to be begging for it.

"This night has been perfect. You are perfect." She breathes, snuggling into me.

I'm not. Far from it, actually. But for her, when she looks at me like she does, I want to be.

T hey come for me a couple weeks after Christmas.
I'm at home during one of the first days Kennedy goes back to school after winter break, just goofing around. With football season over and my community college courses, English Lit and Sports Sciences Throughout History, I don't have much to do. I spent every minute of Kennedy's winter break with her and am bummed she's back in classes.

But that's how they find me on a random Wednesday morning. In my house, in sweatpants, about to start a marathon of a season of *The Office* I never watched.

The knock comes at the door, which in hindsight I should have thought was odd, but I've been a civilian for a couple of months and I'm not as alert.

I should have been, though.

When I swing the door open, a protein bar in my hand, I nearly drop it. Standing on the front porch are two Marines, decked out in their dress blues. They're high-ranking, you can tell by the eagles and stars marking their uniforms.

"Corporal Everett Brock?" the big, burly one asks.

"That's me." I stand up straighter, not able to do anything about the sloppy clothing I have on.

Guys like this are meant to intimidate, and they're doing a hell of a good job. Caught me off guard, at home, in my sweats. I couldn't be at more of a disadvantage.

"We're from the Marine Corps Criminal Investigation Division, just following up on your initial interview after escape."

This guy, the second guy, has a kinder tone and is slimmer, less intimidating. But his eyes, a white blue that is too clear to not seem creepy, they tell just how dangerous he is.

"I told the other investigators everything they needed to know." I scowl, because it's strange that they'd need more information.

And, I suspect, this isn't a friendly call. *Whatsoever.*

"Can we come in?" I still haven't let them in, and the burly one is practically growling.

I notice they haven't given me their names, which is another tactic. If I ask for them, they'll only grill me harder. Better to appear nonchalant, like I have nothing to hide. I know how certain members of the military operate. I learned that part very quick. It's just that being home, I let my guard down too much.

Time to get back up to speed. "Sure."

I step back and then turn, letting them follow me into the dining room. It's the room with the least amount of windows, so no one can see them in here. Not that they won't notice the official vehicle in the driveway. At least Kennedy isn't home and won't be able to question me about this.

I wouldn't be able to tell her a word of it.

The slim one speaks as we sit. "You told the initial investigators that you were detained while doing a check of the site where the mission was to take place?"

"Yes," I answer simply.

"Did anyone deploy you to do that?" he asks.

"Yes."

I'm not going to get verbose, or implicate myself. And even though I appear calm and cool, or at least I hope I do, my heart is hammering in my chest. I know why they're here, that there are holes in my story. That the mission was abandoned after the US military supplies were taken, with me, after I was found by the enemy.

But they'll never be able to prove it was my fault that the mission went south, or never happened. Or at least I think they aren't able to.

"I understand you were close to a number of villagers?" the slim one asks, his eyes unfocused. Or maybe they're just too light to read properly.

I bristle, and he knows he's hit a nerve. "What does that have to do with anything?"

The burly one snorts. "Count on a newb to fall in love with the villagers. You do know we're there to shoot them when they fall out of line, right?"

Under the table, my hands ball into fists. Actually, our presence in the Middle East or any other war zone is to protect the people, the *villagers*. It's to protect innocent people, not just our own, from being slaughtered by their own government. To keep the women and children just trying to make a better life for themselves *alive*.

But I don't say any of this to him. I stay silent, prompting their next question.

"Tell me again why you were at the sight of the HMX?" slim guy asks.

This is where he expects to catch me in a lie. Little does he know, I had three hundred and sixty-five days in a hole to perfect my story. In case I ever got out. In case I didn't completely die out there in that fucking desert.

"I was doing a perimeter sweep, checking into the route for

the mission we were going to execute. I was sent for reconnaissance, to scope out the area. The HMX had been placed a day prior, as was the detail of the mission." I don't go into specifics, because a good soldier would never talk about his op even if it was to high-ranking Marines. "The HMX was secure. The village was fine, no commotion, and I was about to leave by foot to make it back to our base camp. I was jumped from behind by three, maybe four men, and a bag was shoved over my head. After that, I had no chance. My weapon was taken, and they dragged me off before I could do anything."

I don't tell them why I was really there. That I almost blew my fucking hand off before militia found me out.

There are minutes, maybe hours, of deafening silence. I'm not sure how long really, but it feels like years. Sweat trickles down my spine, but I keep stone still. Can't let them see me sweat.

"Funny, not one of your fellow Marines can recall you being told to go on a reconnaissance mission," the burly one tells me, eyeing me suspiciously.

He wants me to break, to squeal under the pressure. What they don't remember is that I've been through far worse. That I kept state secrets, I kept loyal to my country, even when a man was lighting my hair on fire with a blow torch.

"Did those same Marines tell you how I kept my mouth shut for a year in a prison camp. A camp that, if given a choice, you'd pick death rather than to enter?"

They exchange a look and then stare at me for what seems like way too long. I school my features, not even daring to blink. They may rank higher, they may be in a position to knock me down, but I've been in cockfights far deadlier than this.

"We'll be in touch," the bigger guy says, his expression unreadable.

The minute they walk out the door, I go into a full-blown panic.

I should have known all along. I've been lazy, I got comfortable. In my hometown, with my girl. I let myself relax and my mind be eased. I thought I could come back to real life and make something for myself.

I should have known that the sins of my past were coming back to haunt me. That if it wasn't those fucking enemy forces trapping me in a hole, it'd be the military of my own country, the one I was about to betray, that caught up with me.

It's over, the life I have here. I have to get out before I hurt the people I love.

Before I drag Kennedy down with me.

When I step out of my car in the driveway, Everett is waiting for me.

I can see him, deep in thought, sitting on a rocking chair on his back patio. I haven't seen him there since the first day we spoke when he returned home, and my stomach dips a little seeing his brow so furrowed.

Or maybe it dips because of the envelope burning a hole in my back pocket. No, not my college acceptance letter, although I'm still constantly worrying about that.

No, this letter is the one that was never delivered to him. The one that contains those three *major* words I've always wanted to say, and thought I had, until the letter was mailed back to me.

After Winter Wonderland, his admission to me about being a virgin—I still think I'm dreaming when I picture his face in that moment. I never imagined in a million years that we would be able to lose it to each other, that when we do have sex, it will have only ever been with each other. There is something so special in that, but it ascribes even more pressure to the moment. Which is why I wasn't ready.

But I think I am now. We've been together for longer, and once I tell him I'm in love with him, and hopefully he says it back, then I'll truly be ready. It might be cliché to say I need to be in love to have sex, but I've waited this long and I'm a traditional person.

So, I'm finally ready to give him the letter, and then give him *myself*.

"Hey you." I smile as I walk into his backyard.

Everett brings his head up slowly, as if he's so lost in his brain that he didn't even hear me park my car. "Hey."

Something feels off about his mood, but he gets this way sometime. I know he isn't fully healed, that his PTSD may never fully go away. There are good days and bad days. But I try my best to be supportive, to be what he needs.

And what I need right now is to help him, and maybe this letter will do the trick. For both of us.

"Kennedy, we need to—"

I cut him off, barely hearing him because my nerves are hammering in my eardrums. "I have something for you."

Without further talk, I whip the envelope out of my back pocket, the edges frayed and weathered. I've folded it in my hands for the past year, contemplating opening it. I never did, and now I'm glad it's intact for his eyes only.

Everett takes it from me as I sit down beside him, his eyes guarded as he glances at me.

"Read it," I say, prompting him with a tilt of my chin.

His eyes scan the page, and I know what they're seeing.

Everett,

It's been almost a month since I've heard from you. I'm scared. I hope you're all right, that you're just on a mission and you can't write me at the moment. I lie awake at night, praying and hoping that the next day, I'll open the mailbox to one of your letters.

Life isn't right without knowing you're there on the other end of the pen. I miss your corny jokes, or the random pictures from magazines you send. I miss updating you on my life here, and I miss hearing about the line cook's antics at base camp.

Most of all, though, I miss the way you tell me what life will be like when you get home. How we'll be together, or that I'll finally get that kiss you promised. It better be stellar, by the way, with the way you're talking it up! All the time I think about you coming to visit me at college, or finally getting out of Brentwick and being the people we want to be, together.

I'm not sure if you'll get this. I'm really worried, Everett. Please come home to me. All of this is to say, if this is the one letter you receive for a while, I want to say it all. And I've known for a while now, even if we've never kissed, what my feelings are.

I love you, Everett Brock. I have since I can remember. Now, come home, so I can tell you in person.

Please, if you get this, even if you don't feel the same, write me back. I want to know that you're safe.

Come home,

Kennedy

I hold my breath, knowing he's reached the last line. Everett gasped, ran a hand through his hair, and slumped into the rocker as he read the letter. My admission might be shocking to him, but I'd like to think it's not. We both know how we feel.

Hope springs in my chest like brand new flowers trying to reach the sun, and a smile breaks out on my lips. This is the moment, the one I've been waiting for since I wrote those words down on paper. With this declaration out in the air between us, we can finally be together, no unspoken words between us.

"I can't do this." He folds the letter, hands it back.

"Wha ... What?" I must have not heard him right.

Everett's green eyes, the ones that have been so open and

genuine lately, seem to shutter close. "While those words are nice, and I know you mean them, I don't feel the same way."

It feels like someone just took a pickaxe to my heart and tapped the center, sending thousands of tiny spider cracks running all over the organ.

"Yes, you do," I say through the tears forming in my throat.

He shakes his head. "No, I don't. I thought that after years of flirting around the idea, and writing about it, that I'd give it a go. But what we have just doesn't measure up to the hype. I'm not as into it as I thought I'd be."

Each callous, horrible word feels like another slam of a fist down onto that axe. Pieces of my heart start chipping away, falling into the dark abyss.

"You don't mean that."

Every part of me that still holds an ounce of hope and rational thought thinks that he's just lying. That Everett is running scared, that he doesn't want to fight through the hard days to be with me. But the overwhelming majority of me, the one that has been put on his back burner for years, or worse, rejected, knows he has to be telling the truth.

How could I have been so stupid? How could I, once again, fall in love with the boy next door when he can never love me back?

"I do, Kennedy. It's unfortunate, but I just ... I don't want you anymore." He shrugs, as if this means absolutely nothing to him.

And my heart shatters. I'm not even sure if it's there anymore. My hand flings out, reaching for the letter, and grabbing hold to one end.

As I go to stand, intending to take it back and run from him, the paper rips in half.

Everett is holding one half, the one with my most personal feelings written on them, and I hold the other.

Tears begin to slide down my cheeks and I know I need to get out of here. Away from him.

I don't look back as I retreat, knowing that if I do, I'll see the man who holds half my heart, sitting there watching me go.

The sad chords of Maddie & Tae's "Die From a Broken Heart" fills my earbuds, as the thousandth tear slips from the corner of my eye.

As they sing about the utter devastation from a relationship ending, I feel like my chest is breaking open. If I looked down right now, from where I lie on my bed staring at the ceiling, I wouldn't be surprised to find a heart-shaped hole.

Everett has been gone for close to six weeks, and I'm still not anywhere near over it. I probably will never be, at this rate, since I can't do much more than go to school, EMT shifts, and then come home and cry to sad country songs.

The day after he told me he didn't love me back, his car was gone from the Brock's driveway. I thought maybe he was just away for a few days, maybe a week. But then another couple of days would pass, and then a week, and some more weeks ...

He's not coming back.

What makes everything that much worse is that I don't even know where he went. I've called, I've texted. Like a desperate, heartbroken girl, I thought that one day he'd return any of them.

He never has. I thought about driving to find him, but then realized he left word with no one where he's going.

Well, that's not true. He probably told his parents, but I can't very well walk over there and ask them. I'm mortified just living next door, looking into his bedroom window at night knowing he won't be looking back.

I'm devastated, as I knew I would be when our relationship inevitably blew up in my face. What I should have been protecting myself from all along, I instead took a shot at. Because I wanted it so badly that I ignored all the warning signs. I wanted him so much that even as he was telling me he felt nothing, I was trying to prove otherwise.

I feel like a fool. I can barely talk to my friends at school and have been absent for most of the memory-making senior year moments in the last six weeks.

I must not hear the knock at my door, because before I know what's happening, Mom is walking in. Her lips move, but all I hear is Dylan Scott's voice singing in my ears.

"What?" I sit up, clearing my throat from the tears and pulling out an earbud.

"I just wanted to come check if you were joining us for dinner."

Her eyes are so sad, so sympathetic and full of pity, that I have to turn away from her. I pretend to fiddle with my phone on the bed, weighing whether I'm actually hungry today.

"Come down, Kenny. I made chicken cutlets, your favorite." There is so much false hope in her voice.

I know she's putting on, that she's trying to pull me out of my funk. Mom has been trying for weeks to no avail; making my favorite food, asking me to go to the movies, offering retail therapy shopping trips. Not only have I not really accepted any of the invitations, but I have no motivation to go anywhere.

"I'm good. I'll just have some later." My voice sounds hollow and broken.

The weight of Mom sitting on the bed jostles me, and I look over at her. She brushes a stray lock from my cheek, one that probably needs a good wash but I just don't care to try.

"Sweetheart, you will get through this." She nods as if she knows.

Immediately, I burst into tears. I can't hold it in, I can't be strong. Every inch of me feels so fragile, like I'll cave in on myself at the snap of a finger.

"Oh, honey, come here." Mom gathers me in her arms, rubbing my back as I dissolve into sobs on her shoulder. "Talk to me. Talk it out. I swear, it helps."

After wiping away my snot and tears, I blink up at her.

"I feel like I'm breaking, Mom. How could he do this to me? How will I ever trust someone again? Or even want to be with someone. Everett, he's ... I will never feel for someone the way I feel about him."

In this moment, I feel completely hopeless. I know many people say young love feels like a fireball to your soul, that it burns bright but fizzles quickly. That's not what we had, though. I waited years to be with him, and he even told me he waited for me. Wanted me to be his first. All the things he wrote to me, the things he'd said and done over the past months, I know that those were not the actions of a high school crush or someone only in it for the short term.

What we share feels monumental, it spans years and continents. I know, deep in my heart, I'll never find that with someone else.

I fear I'll be alone for the rest of my life.

"I know it feels like that now. And I know we don't know Everett's reasons for leaving, or why he did so in such a brutal way. You feel like you can't possibly put your heart back together, that it will hurt forever. It might, I know how deep your connection was to each other. But in time, it will lessen. The agony will turn to a sting, and then to an ache. Someday, you'll only think about him in passing, and sadness will come with that. But, someday when you least expect it, you will feel happy about your time with him. You'll learn from this, from the good times and the pain now. You'll be stronger because of it. And you'll open your heart to love again, even though it feels impossible now. You will get through this, Kennedy."

Her words equate to a drop in a bucket, something I can't hear right now because they don't ring true. I can appreciate the message she's trying to send, how she's trying to parent. But this heartbreak feels like a permanent eclipse.

Still, I know what part I need to play.

"Thanks, Mom." I lean in to hug her, and it does make me feel marginally better. "I think I will join you for dinner.

Maybe if I fake feeling better, then I actually will *be* better.

Except with every step I take, with each vibration of movement through my body, my heart splits a little further. I have no idea how I'm going to get through this.

Almost two months after Everett leaves, in the middle of March, the letter finally comes.

I've already gotten into my three fallback schools, which really aren't fallbacks but to me rank lower than my top choice. It has the best nursing program, the campus I love, and is far enough away that I can establish a bit of independence.

So I've been waiting, impatiently, for something to go right in my life. Because I need some sort of future that holds promise, that holds possibility.

I still think about him all the time, but Mom was semi-right. In the past month, the pain has dulled a little. Though, not to the point where it doesn't stab at me and wake me in the middle of the night. I can't go days without thinking about Everett, or even hours. He's constantly there, his cold expression on the day he left haunts me awake from my sleep. He still hasn't returned my calls or texts, and no one around town seems to know where he is.

There is no way I can even consider any of the other guys at school, though Logan Myers is still trying. My friends are sympathetic, but they also want me to pick a prom date and go back to being the old Kennedy. The fun, albeit responsible, friend who wanted to make senior year count.

I just don't think I'll ever get back to her, or at least it doesn't feel like it.

The only thing I can look forward to is getting into my top choice college. I've been checking the mailbox every day, the second I pull into the driveway.

So as I pull in, and see the little red flag that was up on my family's old-fashioned mailbox this morning is now down, my heart begins to pound. It's here, I just know it.

My parents aren't home from work, and I'm glad, since I want to be alone while I open this. It seems like such a significant moment in my life, and I've always been more independent than anything. This is my accomplishment, the one I worked for. I want it to sink in in solitude.

The walk to the mailbox feels a hundred miles long, and as I fish through the envelopes and junk letters as I make my way through the garage inside, I'm frantic. Then, my eyes land on it.

My top choice. The envelope is here.

I set my bag down and shrug out of my coat. Steadying my hands on the counter as I look the envelope square in the face, I imagine feeling a thousand times happier than I am this time next year.

My nails slice the envelope. I pull out the letter. And begin to read.

Oh my God. *Oh. My. God.*

I didn't get in. Oh my God, I ... *I didn't get in*.

Black dots start to cloud my vision, and I know that I'm probably having a panic attack. The world feels like it's getting smaller, colder, and all hope ceases to exist.

It's just one thing after another. Up until this point in my life, it feels like most things have gone my way. Or, I've been in control and worked hard to make them go my way. But the two catastrophic events that have now pummeled me into the earth? They were out of my control.

Maybe that's how I should have always been living. Out of control. Not so responsibly.

Because clearly, it didn't matter anyway.

I feel untethered, like I'm floating outside of what my normal life used to be.

I'm still reeling when I call Rachel, but I need a distraction. I've never been the sort of girl not to deal with my problems head-on, and aside from a few rough EMT shifts, I don't mask pain with alcohol.

But tonight, I need to. "Let's go to Everdeen."

A squeal comes through the other end of the phone. "Oh my God, yes! Genius idea. You want Scott to pick you up anything?"

I love that Rachel is the sort of best friend who doesn't question a spontaneous decision, even though she probably hears the upset in my voice. She's been so caring and kind in her own way through this Everett breakup, as has Bianca. They got me drunk, had candy, and movie marathons, offered to burn pictures of him at a barn party in the bonfire.

"Vodka. I want a lot of vodka."

For all I've been through in this new year, I deserve to go a little crazy.

And drown my problems along with it.

33

About three days after the visit from the burly man and slim guy, I went to talk to Dr. Liu.

I told her I couldn't disclose my op, that I'd been on a mission and it had gone terribly wrong. She didn't push me. When I questioned whether I could spend some time away from Brentwick, maybe at a college, sorting my shit out she'd hesitantly agreed it might be good.

While she told me that running from my problems, from my demons, wasn't the answer, there could be something to experiencing a normal college experience.

I didn't tell her that I was trying to run from the government. That I might be in real danger, whether it be legal or otherwise. I didn't tell her that in order to keep Kennedy, and everyone else I love, safe, I had to leave them all behind. I didn't tell her that an hour after I left her office, I smashed Kennedy's heart into a million pieces.

Two and a half months later, I find myself waking up on the shitty college bunk in an unoccupied room in Graden's fraternity. I'm lucky they even had a bed, much less are allowing me to stay here as a non-student and non-brother. But Graden has some pull and understood the look on my face when I showed up telling him I needed to get away from Brentwick.

"Morning, douche breath." Someone wraps on the door, and it sounds like Graden's frat brother, Riley.

This house is loud, disgusting, often crowded and you have to scrounge for food. I've been sitting in on some of Graden's business courses, to see if college is for me, and thus far I'm unimpressed. I'm unimpressed with everything about campus life, but at least it isn't home.

At least I don't have to answer questions that people don't want answers to.

Not that it matters anymore. I broke Kennedy's heart for nothing, or so it seems. A month after they visited my house, the Marine Corps Criminal Investigation Division settled their investigation. It seems that the American government doesn't want to openly admit they were about to bomb a village full of innocent people, and so they can't tie me to tampering with the mission because it would go sideways on them as well.

I walk away with my silence paid for by fully intact military benefits, and no one speaks of what happened for the rest of time. My discharge is honorable, but the military wants to erase that I ever existed in their ranks.

I should go back for her, explain ... but I can't. What happens when the next person comes after me. If the enemy who held me captive finds me. A lot crazier shit has happened in this fucked-up world, trust me I know firsthand, and I don't want Kennedy anywhere near that.

"Party tonight. We need you to pick up sherbet for the jungle juice and Jell-O for the shots." Graden pops his head in, then promptly pops back out.

Part of my agreement of living here is running errands no one else wants to or has time to run.

Another party? That's no surprise. And I can't even be pissed off about it.

Drinking myself to numbness is my favorite pastime these days.

———

"**K**EG STAND!"

A high-pitched girl's squeal rains over the party, and I cringe, taking another sip of my whiskey. I should just start drinking out of the bottle at this point, that's how annoyed these people make me. Giggling and yelling and just generally being obnoxious.

Graden's friends probably would have been the type of guys I hung out with back in the day, but now they just seem like assholes. The girls are too obvious, too sloppy.

The only good thing about these parties is that there seems to be endless alcohol, and that's on my menu.

I've had about three whiskey and ginger ales so far, so my buzz is coming on but not fast enough. This week has been particularly hard with missing Kennedy, and I just want to blur the vision of her in my head.

Walking through the party, where pairs are making out or grinding in time to the music, and one dude is about to puke all over the floor, I sip and try to get in the mood.

Then, just as I pass the living room of the giant house, my eyes lock on something. And this is either the worst nightmare I've ever had or the best dream.

Because standing across the frat house, in a stark white crop top and the tightest black jeans I've ever seen, is Kennedy.

She sees me in the same moment, our gazes an unbreakable line across the room. At first, she rears back, a small *O* forming on her lips. She looks confused, or stunned, but that quickly fades to hurt, and then anger.

Raw, vicious anger.

Jesus Christ, is she stunning. When I look at her, I feel like it's been decades instead of a few months. That's how much I've missed her.

Even like this, even knowing I should stay away from her, we can't help the explosions of chemistry between us. They aren't sparks, they're much more than that. The kind of detonations that destroy lands, cause loss of life.

And if I allow myself to get closer to her, she'll lose her heart.

It appears I have no choice though, since in about three seconds flat Kennedy is marching across the room. She shoves aside drunk girls and the guys playing beer pong to get to me.

"This is where you've been all this time?" She's seething, and I smell the vodka on her breath.

No hi, no nice to see you. Although why would she say those things? Maybe I expected her to be her reasonable self, but with what I did to her and how I left, I shouldn't expect that either.

I should walk away, hide out somewhere else on campus. But, there isn't a reason to avoid her anymore. And God knows I want to take her up to my flimsy bunk and kiss all the pain away between us. But I'm not doing this in the middle of this ridiculous, loud party.

Taking her by the elbow I walk us through the rooms and out to the backyard.

"Don't touch me!" She wrenches away as soon as we step off the deck, into the darkness of the tree line.

"I didn't want to have this conversation in there." I try to put an apology in my tone.

"Why? You didn't want to shout out to the world that you're just not that into me?" Every word of Kennedy's is a dagger.

"Kennedy, please, I never should have—" All I want to do is explain, to wrap my arms around her.

But she cuts me off. "You disappeared, Everett! After wondering before in my life if you were even alive, you thought it was cool to just leave and not even let me know if you were dead!"

She's hysterical, and I know it's part alcohol, but I'm to blame for this hurt. And she's not done.

"If you didn't see me tonight, would you have ever come back? Would you have ever explained? Or is it only because I showed up unexpectedly, that I stumbled into your path, that now you want to talk? I always make it so easy, Everett. So easy for you to break my heart."

A tear rolls down her high, olive cheek bone. I move to swipe it with my thumb, but she backs away.

"Do I really mean nothing to you? After all of it?" Her face falls.

And for as damaged as my own heart has been, I now know I messed hers up worse. What I said to her, it shreds me every time I think about it. Even if it was necessary at the time.

"I never meant a damn word of what I said." I hold my head up high, because now I can finally tell her the truth.

What happens next is *nothing* I ever expected.

Kennedy cracks her palm across my face, the sound of the slap resounding in the dark.

Holy shit, she just slapped me.

Kennedy's finger is in my face in the next minute.

"You have tossed me and my feelings around for the last time, Everett Brock. I told you I was in love with you, and you stared me in the face and said you didn't feel it back. You and your secrets, the things you keep hidden, have ruined me for the last time. I may not be okay for a long time, but at least I won't have to live in the purgatory you forced me into. Screw you, Everett Brock."

She takes off, but I stay hidden in the tree line, my cheek stinging.

I underestimated just how badly I hurt her, and for that I'm a fool. I've been so focused on hardening my heart, on morphing back into the injured, broody soldier who came home all those months ago, that I forgot to feel. I forgot to realize just how tragically I broke her heart. How I broke my own.

Tonight, Kennedy is furious and fuming with alcohol-induced confidence.

But, tomorrow, that's my chance. I have to pull out all the stops.

Including the letter that tells her exactly what her letter told me.

I wake up in a fog of vodka, arguments, and heartbreak.

"Fuck *me*." Bianca groans beside me, both of us stuffed into the frame of a twin bed.

We're sleeping in some random dorm room of a friend of a friend of Scott's. He and Rachel are on a futon in the next room, and we heard them having drunk, sloppy sex last night. Which was *gross*.

"I think I'm going to throw up," I say, as the room spins.

I slap a hand over my eye, willing the light to go away.

"You went so freaking hard last night. I'm so proud." She rolls over, snuggling me.

A huge weight jumps on us, and it lets out an *oomph*. "I'm proud, too. But I'd be prouder if I also had a breakfast sandwich from McDonald's. My stomach hates me."

Rachel wedges herself in between us, and her elbow stabs me in the gut. "Hey! Watch it. You're going to make me toss up last night's ... ugh"

I can't even say the word vodka without dry-heaving.

"You went H.A.M after we left that frat party." Rachel chuckles, snuggling her nose right up to my cheek.

She wants to be lovey dovey in the morning, while all I want to do is get some blackout curtains and Advil.

"Oh God, I don't even remember how we got home." I rub my temples.

"Well, we basically carried you up the stairs. You were pissed after your fight with ..." Bianca trails off.

Images of last night come back in hazy, blurred scenes. The parties, the drinks, and ...

"Oh shit, *Everett*." Dread fills my stomach, and I really think I'm going to hurl now.

Rachel points her finger up to the ceiling. "AND, *bingo!*"

My heart is racing now as I shoot straight up in the twin bed, shifting all three of us. Shit, shit, shit. I completely forgot, thanks to the alcohol I downed because of said fight, that I saw Everett last night.

And then my hand clamps over my mouth. "*Oh my God.* Did I slap him?"

"Yep." Bianca cackles. "I wish I could have seen it, but you were bragging about it so hilariously that I almost feel like I was there."

I'm freaking out. Internally, it feels like I'm going to poop out my heart. Tears form in the back of my throat. My hands begin to sweat.

"What did I do?" I whisper.

Rachel sits up, slinging her arms around my shoulders. "What needed to be done a long time ago. Everett has tossed you about for years, bringing you up so high and then slamming you back down. I've seen you torture yourself over the past few months because he left. He deserved to be screamed at. He deserved the slap."

She's probably right, but I still feel horrible.

Bianca clears her throat. "But, if you did want to clear the whole mess up, he's been sleeping on a bench outside the dorm since three a.m."

"What?" I screech.

They both nod, and Rachel speaks first. "Yep. You needed to give him the smackdown, but man do I love a good grovel. The boy found out where we were staying and has been blowing my phone up since the wee hours of the night. So, if you want to hear him out, he's downstairs."

Do I want to hear him out? Aside from the fact that I could toss the contents of my stomach up in two minutes, and I probably look like crap, I do want to talk to Everett. There are so many things left unknown, left unsaid. And I'd be lying if I said I didn't still think he was my end game.

Like I'd told Mom, and my friends, on various occasions; Everett and I had something deeper than just the first time puppy love. I have never felt one ounce of what I feel for Everett for any other boy. I don't think I ever will. So if it takes us sitting down to talk this out, to discuss how much he's hurt me and how we move forward, then I want to do it.

"You have to help me look like I didn't just die in a bottle of vodka," I tell my friends.

Twenty minutes later, I have a halfway decent outfit of jeans and a sweater on, a face of brief makeup, my hair has been braided by Bianca, and Advil aids in the process of my terrible headache subsiding.

When I walk outside, the sun beaming bright in my face and a cool late March breeze blowing, I immediately spot him. He's stretching on a park bench not five feet from the entrance of Scott's friend's dorm. It's completely unfair that even when sleeping drunk on a goddamn wooden bench, he looks practically edible.

Everett doesn't see me yet, and I take the opportunity to pump myself up. He's too disarming, too gorgeous, and I let that wash over me and then push it away. I can't be swayed by how affected I am by him, because there are serious things we need to talk about. I need to be strong, to be the Kennedy that everyone else knows me to be.

"Everett," I speak up, catching his attention.

Those green eyes snap to me, all smoldering and still full of hazy sleep. "Oh, thank God."

I feel the puzzled look that falls over my face. "What?"

He looks me up and down, as if he's checking for damage. "I spent half the night trying to call you and your friends, or find you at parties. I walked all over campus. I had these horrible visions of you ending up somewhere, drunk in a ditch."

I cross my arms over my chest. "Funny, the things you imagine when somebody just up and leaves without another word."

My message is heard loud and clear as Everett sighs. "Kennedy, I'm sorry. I should have told you I was all right. That I was safe. I just ... I didn't know how to keep in contact without wanting to come back to you."

I sit down beside him, the electric force always present between us, but I keep my distance. "Why would you not want to come back to me? What was so awful, what did I do that was so wrong—"

"No, *no*. You did nothing wrong. You're, everything about you is perfect. Sometimes I don't even believe just how good and wonderful you are. It's me, Kennedy. There are things I can't tell you, or couldn't tell you. Things that would be dangerous to you if you knew. Or, and this is so selfish of me, would make you look at me differently."

I slap my palms against my jeans. "I'm not sure how much clearer I could have been, Everett. I don't care about what you did. I mean, I care about it. I want to know. But nothing you could say would make me not love you. I told you I love you, Everett. And you ran."

When he turns his eyes to me, they're so sad, my heart breaks a little more. "It destroyed me to do that to you. It feels like there are just a thousand knives lodged in my heart at all times. Of course, I feel the same. I was a coward, but you have to believe me. I was protecting you, too."

My heart begins to beat again, under his spell as it's always been. Is he telling the truth? And does he really love me, too?

"The reason I was captured in the first place ... it was my fucking fault. I-I did something. Unforgivable, but I wouldn't be able to live with myself if I didn't."

There is desperation in his voice, like he wants to tell, like he's right on the edge. I grab his hand, my eyes intense on his. "You can tell me, Everett. Let me carry this with you."

He shakes his head, like he's deciding against it. The root of all of our problems were the secrets he carried home. Maybe if they can be brought into the light, we'll be able to move forward.

"Will you go somewhere with me? We can't, not here," he says, looking around.

Students have begun to wander out of their Sunday morning dorm caves in search of greasy breakfast foods. Our conversation isn't private anymore, and I know that I shouldn't even put up a fight. I want to know the things he is going to tell me. I'm not foolish enough to stick to stubborn pride or hard-to-get plans.

"Yes," I answer simply.

He leads and I follow, and I don't know yet if that's into the darkness or the light.

EVERETT

My hands rotate around the steering wheel as I pull onto the gravel road.

I feel Kennedy's eyes on me, and I know she's questioning where I'm taking her. We're probably not in the best of places in our relationship for me to take her out into the woods, but I want to have this conversation out here.

When Kennedy took my hand back on the Everdeen campus, I wanted to shake my head. Because she can't know, that's always been the rule. I've already said too much. And yet …

I'm ready to tell her. To get this fucking gorilla of a secret off my chest. To not carry it as my cross to bear anymore. Even if someone else tries to come for me, for us, at least there will be nothing between us any longer.

"Where are we going?" she finally asks, after being silent most of the car ride.

"You'll see in a second," I tell her as the car winds down the unpaved path.

I found this spot when I was out driving around one day, having been fed up with the fraternity house and needing silence. We come to the end of the path, and the trees open up to the shore of a lake, surrounded by mountains.

"Wow." She breathes, looking around.

"Yeah. I found it one day when I wasn't even looking for it. I think it must be used as a fishing spot, but I've never seen anyone out here. Come on."

I grab a blanket from the back and Kennedy follows me down to the shore, where the water laps a few yards away. Spreading it out, I sit and she thankfully sits beside me. A hush of silence falls over us as we watch the water, and I know I should just jump right into it. Gulping in a deep breath and steeling my heart, I start.

"I was being trained for a very special sect of the Marines. As a black ops soldier, the kind of guys who do things so fucking evil, they probably aren't legal under any international law. I was hesitant going in, after all, I was only a rookie compared to most of the guys. But my sniper shooting couldn't be matched, and I have a thing for maps."

Kennedy interrupts, her observation invading the moment. "I remember when you drew that insane senior treasure hunt for your grade."

The memory makes me smile. "That was some of my best work. Anyway, they were training me. The missions were top secret and fucking crazy. I can't go into much detail, but I never thought I would be doing some of the things I was doing. The base camp I was stationed at, it was near a village. As a soldier, I still had to do regular sweeps of the area, along with my training. You get to know the people. They bring you food, the kids want to play sports with you, and a lot of them are happy to have the protection. They fear for their lives against the terrorist organizations and militia that run rampant in the areas. I became close to them, which in hindsight was a terrible mistake but it's hard not to."

I feel her leaning in, listening to every word, but I don't dare look at her.

"I got the orders that we were going on a mission. That explosive materials had been dropped in and we were to bomb the village our base camp was situated near."

Kennedy gasps, and I can see her hand fly up to cover her mouth.

"There was intel of an underground terrorist cell operating in the village, one that we'd missed had the potential to cause catastrophic damage. So we were ordered to take it out. Everyone in the village. No warning. It was off the books, obviously Americans would go apeshit if they knew we were murdering innocent women and children, even if it was for the greater good. I just … I couldn't go through with it. These were people I'd laughed with, who attempted to teach me the language, I played ball with the sons and daughters. I couldn't do it, Kennedy. So, in the middle of the night, about twelve hours before the mission was set to go down, I snuck out to the HMX—the explosive materials. I thought if I could move it, or hide, or hell, I had no plan other than to save those people's lives. But I ended up making too much noise, at one point I thought I'd activated one and that it would explode, I don't know what happened. Next thing I know, I'm discovered by enemy forces, so I guess there was a cell operating in the village. They threw a bag over my head, and I assume they took the HMX with them because next thing I know, I wake up in a hole in the ground and I'm being tortured as to what it was supposed to be used for."

I'm silent after that, thinking about the whole situation. "I'm the reason I was a prisoner of war. It was my own fault. And I put valuable American war materials in the hands of dangerous people."

"You saved the lives of those villagers." Kennedy shakes her head when I finally look at her.

"I betrayed my country." I let my head fall, picking at the strands of the blanket we sit on.

Two of her fingers come up under my chin, pushing upward until our eyes are just inches apart. "You are a hero. You followed what your gut told you was the right thing to do, and you saved those people."

Hope flutters through my heart. "You aren't ashamed of me?"

"How could I be ashamed of the type of man who would go against an order to save innocent lives?" She looks so sincere, I could cry.

"It's something I struggle with every day." I break down, all vulnerability on the line now. "Did I do the right thing? What did that terrorist cell end up doing with the explosives? I might have saved those people, but look what happened to me. And then, my own government tried to turn against me."

"What?" Kennedy asks, confused.

I grasp her fingers from my chin and lace our hands together on the blanket. I can't stand not touching her any longer.

"The reason I left was because days prior, two Marines showed up at my door while you were at school. They were from the investigations division, had all of these questions about why I was by the HMX that night, tried to poke holes in my story. They know I'm lying. Still do, even though it's dismissed because this country doesn't want to admit what it was about to do. I didn't want you caught up in all of it. If anyone came after me, be it this country or someone else I'd never forgive myself if you were hurt in the process. I care too much about you. That's why I left. Why I couldn't tell you. Why I had to pretend like I wasn't cutting out my own heart."

Her eyes harden for a second. I know it's a lot to digest, but everything I have hangs on this moment.

"How do I know you're not just saying all of this? That you would have eventually come back for me? That you actually do feel the same?" There is so much fear in her eyes.

I pull the envelope from my sweatshirt, and hand it over. "There is nothing I can say to make you believe me. So I guess you'll just have to see for yourself."

Kennedy examines the envelope, looks at the red stamp blaring on the front of it. I know that as she slices it open and removes the letter, she sees the date at the top. Three days before I was taken.

Kennedy,

This letter is going to be short, so I apologize. Something is happening, and I can't say more. But I wanted to say something before it did.

I love you. I've loved you from the moment I saw you skin your knee on your bike when you were six years old. I've been an idiot, waiting this long and never daring to tell you how I felt in person, but here it is.

Wait for me. I'm coming home for you.

-Everett

Kennedy blinks up at me, wonder and emotion in her eyes.

I shrug, squeeze her hand. "It looks like we both had the same idea. That we needed to leave no big words left unsaid. It just it took a while for those words to get to each other."

"You felt this way all along." She breathes, her eyes searching mine.

"I've loved you from the very start." I nod.

"And I love you," she returns.

It's that simple. All the cards are out on the table, and in the end, we want to be together.

I'm done with waiting. My hands reach for her at the same

time Kennedy leans in, and my fingers run through her wavy tendrils at the exact moment our lips meet.

The kiss is gentle, searching, but also searing. It's the first one that has no truths hiding between it.

Finally, Kennedy has mixed her light with my dark, and it feels right for the first time in forever.

"So, tell me about the last month."

Dr. Liu sits across from me in her office, and I marvel at just how much more comfortable I am in here than I was the first time I came for a visit.

And not just in here, but in life. Since I shared the whole story with Kennedy, since we talked about how I left and everything we'd been holding back from each other, I've felt lighter. With the military off my back, and the investigation settled, I could really throw myself into healing, into therapy. Don't get me wrong, there are still demons every week, sometimes daily, but with the support around me and with Dr. Liu's help, I've learned how to cope better.

"Well, you know I've been helping Kennedy through the whole college thing."

A couple days after I packed up my stuff, left the fraternity house, and moved back to Brentwick with my parents, Kennedy told me about not getting into her top choice college.

"How has she been taking it?" Dr. Liu asks.

"At first, not well. She was really upset, kept saying that she'd worked so hard, and how could someone who did all the right things not get in. But we talked it through. She has three other really great choices. And if anything, it's kind of a dose of reality she needed. Not that I'd ever say it to her face. But life isn't perfect, it isn't meant to be. I keep telling her that it's messy, and there could be another choice or plan down the road that involves going to a different school that she might never have considered had she got in."

Dr. Liu looks impressed. "That's very astute of you. And a great way to lift her spirits."

"I'm just trying to be there for her. She stood by me, when she didn't have to, through a lot of crap. She's going to do incredible anywhere she goes, so it's just a matter of being there for her to figure it out."

As for me, college isn't my thing. I learned that much while staying with Graden. And even though I attended my community courses for a minute there, school is over for me. I want to jump into something and learn hands on. I can't sit in a classroom anymore.

"And your relationship, it's good?"

"Great, actually." I don't feel like going into any more detail than that.

But, it's been better than ever. I feel like I can finally let my guard down with Kennedy. Like we're the best friends you're supposed to be as boyfriend and girlfriend. She is the person I feel most comfortable with, the one I want to experience everything with. Last weekend, we drove two hours to a shore town that was just opening its shop doors for the spring. Before that, we had a cooking competition night with her parents, where we beat them in a lasagna cook off and cupcake bakeoff. Kennedy came to my grandparent's house for Easter, and I have a plan to ask her to prom in the works.

"I got a job offer the other day." I bring it up out of the blue, though it's the thing that has most been on my mind.

"Oh?" She sounds interested, but in typical Dr. Liu fashion, she's going to let me talk out the decision.

I nod. "Director of Town Athletics for Brentwick. The pay is good, I'd get to work in sports, which I love. Get to oversee the little league and travel soccer clubs, that sort of thing."

"Sounds like a good fit for you," she comments.

"But ..." I start, and I see Dr. Liu grin, like she knew I'd say that. "I'm not sure I want to stay in Brentwick. Now that I'm clear of the investigation, and things are good with Kennedy, with my parents, I'm not sure I want to stay here. Maybe I'll follow Kennedy. Maybe I'll check out a different state for a while. And I'm not sure that it's the job for me. It's probably a lot of paper-work and dealing with headaches, rather than hands-on."

"If it doesn't feel one hundred percent like a yes when you initially think about it, then maybe taking some space from it is good," Dr. Liu says, giving me that thought to chew over.

She's right. If something in my life doesn't strike me as an absolute yes, I should wait for the thing that does.

The box of donuts I'm carrying is so tempting, I'm about to sneak my hand inside and grab one.

"I know that look. Don't you dare." Kennedy wags a finger at me as she hops off the stool she's sitting on.

It's become a ritual over the last few weeks that I bring her and the EMT crew a box of fresh cider donuts when she's working a shift. I set them down on the table as she and the other three EMTs on shift swarm around the box and then snag my girl by the waist.

"You have to pay the entry fee," I tell her, before bringing my mouth down over hers.

Kennedy sighs and leans into me, and she lets the kiss go as far as me slipping my tongue past her lips, before pushing off my chest.

"Entry fee for donuts? That isn't even a thing." She rolls her eyes.

Nicholas, one of the other EMTs, chuckles. "Unless there is a fee for being horny. Because Everett is definitely that."

I shoot the bird while Kennedy, and her boss, Judy, have their backs turned. But he's not wrong. I am a horny bastard.

Each time I'm around Kennedy, I just can't help myself. Over the past month, we've definitely gotten reacquainted with each other in a bodily sense, and my cock is so aware around her that I can barely leave the house without a semi.

They're all munching away on donuts when the radio crackles, calling in a bunch of codes I can't even begin to comprehend.

"It's from the local sports complex. A kid collapsed while playing basketball. We need to move," Judy tells them, already swinging her gear into the truck.

Damn, they're all so fast. Everyone buzzes around, grabbing medical supplies, bags, and gear. The truck is loaded in two minutes flat, while the team speaks in code to each other. I'm left standing there, feeling the infectious energy moving around but unable to translate it all.

Kennedy appears in front of me. "We have to go to this call. I'm sorry babe, I don't know how long it will take or when I'll be back. I love you."

She leans up and presses a kiss to my lips, but I grab her hand just as she goes to turn, Judy summoning her into the back of the ambulance.

"Let me come with you. I want to see." I know my voice sounds desperate.

But in the last few seconds, it's the first time I've felt the familiar rush that speaks deeply to my soul.

Kennedy looks to Judy, who takes a split second to decide. Her face assesses me, then snaps to seriousness.

"You come, observe. Don't get in the way, and don't try to help. You're not licensed and I shouldn't even be doing this, but as former military, you might be of help. Get in."

Kennedy pulls me in as I jump up, and off we go.

The sirens racing above my head only serve to spread a calmness over my heart. This is what I know. The hectic chaos of trouble, of battle. I know the fear that channels into precision focus. I know the ins and outs of navigating trauma.

Judy goes over protocol and I dial in, trying my best to understand what the rest of the EMTs already know second hand.

And in what feels like exactly one minute, we're arriving at the sports complex. It's a place I've been numerous times over the years, whether it was for recreation league soccer or indoor practices for football in the winter during high school.

"Don't get in the way," Judy scolds me one last time as the back of the ambulance flies open and everyone descends.

I follow, keeping a close distance but careful not to ruin their flow. When we step inside, a frantic parent directs us to which court the kid collapsed on. Everyone is hushed and standing when we get into the arena, trying to see if the kid is breathing.

Judy takes point, hustling over to the seven- or eight-year-old kid in his baggy basketball uniform. He's lying on the floor, unmoving, and I can tell his face is starting to turn blue. Kennedy bends down, removing several items from her kit, when Judy whispers to the team.

"He's not breathing, we're going to have to shock him. Kennedy, start compressions while I get the AED set up."

Kennedy doesn't hesitate, and I watch my girlfriend perform perfect CPR on him. She is relentless and concentrated. At this moment, I'm so in awe of her. I usually am anyway, but I've never seen her in action on the job, and it's a rare treat that I get to be here now.

But something else is wriggling free in my chest. A sense of belonging. Of purpose. I thrive in this chaos.

Judy finally has the AED up and running, and as she attaches the patches of electricity to his chest, I anticipate the next few moments.

They send an electric shock to his heart, and it's like they're waking me up, too.

To what I've been missing. To what I crave.

When the kid finally comes to, heaving out a breath, it feels like I'm breathing for the first time in months.

I watch as Kennedy and the other EMTs strap him to a back board, and load him onto the stretcher. They check his vitals, talk to him.

By the time we make it out to the ambulance, I have my answer.

And it's one thousand percent a yes.

Friday nights look a lot different than they used to.

Before, I would have met up with my best friends to troll the parties in the area, or find something remotely amusing to do. I'd act as fifth wheel while they made out with their boyfriends. Or, I'd beg off plans and stay in my room reading or binging *Gilmore Girls*.

Now, I spend it with Everett, mostly. He takes me out for pizza, or hot wings during half-price appetizers. Sometimes we meet up with my friends, or have dinner with one set of our parents.

But these kinds of nights, like tonight, are my favorite. Spent in my basement, which is finished with my dad's prized projection-screen TV. I get to cuddle up with Everett on the couch, where we pretend to watch TV but really just fool around. His hands slip under my shirt, my fingers drum on his abs, and eventually, clothes start to come off.

Though tonight, I can't get out of my own head. I shrugged Everett off when he tried to unbutton my jeans, saying I just want to watch *Not Another Teen Movie*.

In reality, I'm still really bummed out about how things

shook out for me with college. I have another two weeks to decide which school I'm going to attend, and I feel lackluster about my choices. My heart had been set on my top choice, and now that I don't have the option, I barely want to think about it.

Everett has been so supportive, telling me I'll succeed wherever I go, but that's not the point. I know I should be so happy that I have so many amazing things in my life, but this has been a hard pill to swallow.

If I've learned anything in my senior year though, it's that all the preparing and planning in the world won't help you. I'd banked on Everett coming home way sooner than he had. I thought it would be picture-perfect the moment he came back to Brentwick, sweeping me off my feet. I thought we'd have our happily ever after, and I'd win homecoming queen and ride off into my top college choice sunset.

Life doesn't work that way, though.

"I love you." Everett brushes back a lock of my hair. "You in there? Earth to Kennedy."

God, I love hearing those words. Ever since I read them in his letter, the one that never got delivered to me, I melt each time he says them. I can't believe we both wrote those words, sent them, and had them returned. It's as if the world was biding its time, like it had a plan to bring us together at the exact right time.

I admit, it's taken some time since he came back from Evergreen, but we're more solid than we've ever been. With his admission about what happened overseas, about all the things he's been through, it all made so much more sense. He was trying to protect me, though I wish he'd told me that from the start.

"I love you." I hug him back. "Just thinking about college."

"You're going to make the right choice. It will come. Maybe

just take your mind off of it for a while. Focus on what's right in front of you." He kisses me lightly.

The feel of his mouth on mine sends a tingle down my spine. *Focus on what's right in front of me.*

I've been dancing around losing my virginity for weeks. It seems like every time I make the decision to do so, something gets in the way. Whether it be Everett having a freak out, or me not getting into college, the emotional stress puts the kibosh on thinking about getting physical with him.

Except, I know right now, at this moment. This is what I want. What I need. I'd promised that when there were no more barriers between us, when the feelings had been admitted, secrets had been shared and those three words had been said ... that'd I'd be ready.

It strikes, so hard between my shoulder blades, just how ready I am.

My hands reach up to grab his face, taking it between my hands, and I kiss him with an open mouth. I want to brand him, burn him. And when I pull back, that white hot pleasure already building between my thighs, I know what I want.

"Make love to me, Everett," I whisper, my eyes just an inch from his.

Our noses touch, and his green irises go wide. "You're sure?"

I nod. "Yes. I want to do this with you. Be as close as two people possibly can be."

He leans back in, kissing me with such fervor that I almost can't hold myself upright.

Moving from the couch, Everett takes the blanket we were just lying under and spreads it on the floor. "Your parents?"

"They'll never come down. They never do." I shake my head, too aroused to even care about intruders.

All teenagers do this, right? So what will it matter that this is in my parent's house? I'm in love with my boyfriend who treats me like a princess. They couldn't wish for more.

Once he sets some pillows on the floor and makes it as comfortable as he can, his hand reaches for mine. I join him, allowing him to lead me to kneel in the middle of the blanket.

"I love you so much. I'm so thankful I waited, for it to be you. You're the only woman I've ever seen, Kennedy. The only one who my eyes search for in every room, in every place."

His words slay me, because I can't believe he waited. That we get to give ourselves to each other as equals.

Fingertips toy at the hem of my sweatshirt, and I suck in a lungful of air.

"Is this okay?" his smooth, deep voice whispers.

My nipples bud at his tone, and I scoot forward until I can nod into his shoulder. Slowly, Everett lifts my sweatshirt up and over my head, throwing it behind him. The cool air of the basement hits my bare skin, and I press myself harder into him seeking warmth.

We've been fooling around for months, even before he went to Everdeen, and being naked in front of him doesn't embarrass me like I thought it would. No, Everett makes me feel like a woman, like my skin and body were meant to be adored by him.

He touches me, filling his palms with the cups of my bra, and I come alive like a wire. My thighs clench, and I automatically thrust my chest out. My hands seek to feel his skin, and I pull his shirt up and away.

I've dreamed about this so many times. Being alone with this boy, this man, the one who makes my heart beat out of my chest. How many times have I fantasized about him moving over me, making me feel better than anything I've dreamed before?

In no time flat, we've undressed each other, stealing kisses here and stroking our hands up down the other. Everett in the flesh is breathtaking. All carved muscle and well-honed strength. His scars tell his story, one that only endears him to me more.

"Let me see you." Everett's voice is husky, and his eyes flash a brilliant green as he studies me like the most magnificent piece of art. "You're so beautiful, sometimes it hurts to look at you."

I feel myself blush from head to toe, but I'm not self-conscious. I couldn't be, not with him. Most girls would be uncomfortable, but we know each other so well and I've thought about this moment for forever.

Laying me back, Everett starts to kiss me, not a shred of anything between us. I feel his arousal, the wet tip leaving a trail over my stomach, as he slowly grinds into me. I'm restless and pent up, and I want him to touch the tight bud between my legs so badly that I might be whimpering.

"I want to try something first. To make you feel good, before ..." His voice is sincere, and makes me flush all over again.

Before I know what he's doing, Everett's mouth is between my legs, and I have to slap a hand over my mouth when he licks right up my center.

"Oh my God," I breathe out, hoping that only the two of us heard that.

It's the first time he's done this, the only time a guy has ever gone down on me. That sounds so adult, but the way Everett is licking and sucking me, I can barely think.

With every swirl of his tongue, and the way he's nibbling on that hot button between my thighs, I am so close in a matter of seconds. This feels taboo, which only makes it hotter, and the way I'm exposed should make me feel vulnerable, but instead, I feel wholly powerful.

And when Everett pushes two fingers inside me at the same time his tongue presses down on my clit, I'm a goner. With my eyelids screwed up tight, fireworks start to go off in front of them. I'm shaking, my whole body reduced to shivers and pleasure. The orgasm steals my breath, and my hands latch to his thick blond hair, keeping him there. It's shameful, but he feels so good I can't care less.

As the waves of climax subside, Everett hovers over me, watching my face as it breaks into a smile. He nudges my nose in a loving way, but I'm still amped up even through the haze of my orgasm.

Reaching between us, I feel for him. My hand wraps around his stiff, hot tool, and Everett drops his head to my shoulder.

"I want to feel you," I whisper as I stroke him with my fist.

I'm rewarded with a growl, one that sends shivers up my spine. Just thinking about what we're about to do, how we're about to give ourselves to each other, it wakes up every primal nerve in me. Even though I just came down from my orgasm, my core is alive and clenching again.

Everett reaches for his jeans, where he finds his wallet. I watch as he pulls the condom out, waiting on the blanket in anticipation. Every cell in my body pulses with electric energy, and I see him in shadow art as he rolls the latex onto himself. He's big, and I know how this works but at the same time ... how is this going to work?

He returns to me, positioning himself between my legs. I run my fingers over the stubble on his jaw, trying not to be nervous.

"I love you." His eyes connect with mine.

"I love you." My voice is throaty and anxious.

And then he pushes in. We don't say it will hurt, or that he's sorry for causing me pain. These are things we know. But I'm not ready for the pressure, the sharp, piercing ache that penetrates me as Everett tries to fill me with himself.

I squirm, trying to get away, and the pain burns so fiercely that my eyes start to water.

"Look at me. Look at me, Kennedy." Green eyes blaze into mine.

I try to focus on Everett, to look past the pain. He bends to kiss my jaw, my cheeks, my nose, my lips. Every part of my face, every part of me that he can reach, he kisses. Slowly, as his lips coax pleasure that runs over my skin, I forget about the pain. Slowly, it subsides.

And what it gives way to is out of this world. Being connected to this man, the one I've loved for so long, as he looks down at me like he sees the universe opening for him.

"It feels ... *good*." I breathe, sliding my hands up to his shoulders, feeling his strong arms brace over me.

"*Christ*, it does." He blows out a breath as if he's been holding it for years.

Everett starts to really move then. With every thrust, I have to contain a moan. With every stroke of him in to the very hilt, my legs spread wider. This feeling, one of such pleasure and fullness, now I know what all the fuss is about. He's building me up, taking me higher, and while the pain is still there, I know that in time this will feel *perfect*.

I know I'm about to make noise, and I maneuver his lips to mine, letting him swallow my moans. He pounds into me, letting himself go wild.

"Kennedy," he growls in my ear, and then goes still.

Everett's breathing comes out in puffs, and I turn my face to the side to watch him. He's beautiful, the epitome of a man in this moment. I can't believe we waited for this; I'm so thankful we waited for this.

Once he's emptied himself into the condom, he collapses onto me, running his hands up and down my arms.

I'm still catching my breath, reeling from the raw pleasure, emotion, and intensity that this just evoked, when Everett lifts his head. He's thoroughly sexed, and I know that I'll remember him like this, in this moment, for the rest of my life.

"I'm never leaving you, Kennedy. I am yours. Forever."

"**D**eposit sent."

I sigh, looking around the table at my Mom, Dad, and Everett.

"This is a great choice, honey. Great school, wonderful nursing program. You're going to do amazing. And it's in New York, you'll have the mountains and gorges, it's so beautiful." Mom squeezes my hand across our dining room table.

I nod my head, feeling content with my decision. In the end, I went with my second choice school, which still has one of the best nursing programs in the region. I'll be about three hours from home, which is just far enough and close enough at the same time. Rachel will be two hours away in New York City, and Bianca will be the opposite direction in Pennsylvania, about an hour away.

"You're going to kick—" Everett clips off the end of his sentence, blushing at my dad.

You'd think there was nothing my foul-mouthed Marine could blush at, but apparently gaining my father's approval is top priority. Not that Dad has ever said anything about our relationship; I think he's actually rather relieved we finally worked it out. Drama is not my dad's language.

"It will be great, sweetie." Dad smiles at me.

We've just finished up dinner at my parent's house, Everett was invited for his favorite meatloaf my Mom makes, and we've been talking about the future. For a while there, I was pretty adamant against talking about it, because I was so upset about not getting into my top college.

But my parents, and especially Everett, have been here every step of the way. Something Everett said has been ringing in my brain every time I think about college.

"There could be another choice or plan down the road that involves going to a different school that you might never have considered had you got into your top choice."

And it's so true. Life is messy. Maybe I wasn't meant to get into my top choice, because life had another plan. Just like I had to wait this long for Everett, maybe it was meant to happen this way since we're so happy now.

Now that the decision is made, that I'm into college and I'm on my way to graduation, I can celebrate. I've been looking at pictures of my soon-to-be campus home, the surrounding areas, and getting myself acquainted with the nursing program there. It's really in-depth, and I can't wait to start.

"Do you want to go pick up some ice cream?" Everett asks as we clear the table.

"Sure. Mom, Dad, you want anything?"

"Chocolate!" Mom calls from the kitchen.

"I'll have a mint chocolate chip milkshake, thanks," Dad says as I hear the sink turn on. He always washes.

I lace my hand through Everett's as we head for the door. "Let's go, babe."

The weather has turned warmer as we head into summer, and I love the nighttime breeze. "Do you want to walk?"

Indigo Drive is only about a quarter of a mile from the town's ice cream shop, and it's a nice night.

"Yeah, let's do it, *babe*." Everett smirks at me.

We've been using pet names, since we can now, but more in a sarcastic way than anything. It's fun and flirty and makes the butterflies in my stomach soar. Things with Everett have been so good since he told me about why he left Brentwick. I can't believe he's been through so much strife, and all the pain it's caused him. More and more each day, he seems to be returning to the Everett I knew before. Only better, because now we're so open and vulnerable with each other.

"So, I've been thinking," he starts, his hand swinging mine as we walk. "About what I'll do when you go to college."

A pit forms in my stomach. I've tried to avoid thinking about it, because I don't want to have to leave him again.

"I told you before that I wouldn't leave you again. That's a promise. So, I'm going to come with you."

I completely stop walking and his hand is pulled from mine in the halted motion. "What?"

Everett turns around on the sidewalk, a knowing smile on his lips. He walks back to me and settles his hands on my hips.

"I'm coming with you. I'm going to move to New York, find an apartment, be near you. I can't stand the thought of another second without you. I want you to have the full college experience, but I also can't go months without seeing you. It would be impossible. So, I'm coming with you."

I'm so freaking happy, I could burst out of my skin. "I-I can't believe it. Of course, I want you to come with me. I've been dreading it thinking about saying goodbye. But what will you do?"

"Well, I thought I'd get my EMT certification." He drops it casually, like this isn't the biggest piece of information on our walk.

"What?" I must have heard him wrong.

He nods, grinning from ear to ear. "That night that I went with you and the team out on the call, I haven't felt that *right* in a very long time. The chaos, the sense of purpose and helping those in need. I thrive in that hectic environment, and I think I could be really good at it."

I tilt my head to the side and consider him. Now that I think about it, Everett would make an excellent EMT. "And you wouldn't have to go to school. Just take the course, which is quick enough."

"Exactly, it's all on the job learning, which is how I learn best. I can come with you to New York, too. They need EMTs everywhere."

I smile at him, feeling like all of our puzzle pieces are falling into place. "I think it's the best idea you've had yet."

He tugs on my hand. "Well, you haven't heard my one where I suggest we make out in the park on our way to the ice cream shop."

That makes me laugh, the sound getting lost in the night. "Now you're talking!"

Colors and patterns and glitter can be seen every way you turn, and those are just the dresses.

The music bumps as Rachel, Bianca, and I dance in a small circle in the middle of the floor. I can't believe this is one of the last times we'll be together in the coming months. That it will be one of the last things we do as students at Brentwick High.

When we were freshman, senior prom felt so far away. It's something we always looked forward to, and would highlight dresses in the catalogs every year, but felt so unreachable. We always had more time.

But now, time is running out. There are mere weeks before graduation, and all of our college choices are made.

"It feels fitting that we end this thing called high school with a massive party. Who doesn't love a ball gown?" Rachel smiles as she slings her arms around both of us.

She's wearing a sexy red mermaid gown, while Bianca opted for a leopard print A-line that looks incredible. I went with a deep maroon silk dress with a plunging back. Everett keeps trying to sneak his hands down there, and I kind of love that it's making him like a dog chasing a bone.

"I love you, guys," I say simply.

"What, no Kennedy speech? You're usually the educated, long rambling one." Bianca giggles.

"I just ... this is perfect. I can't imagine a better night than this to cap off a great year," I say.

It was great. There were so many speed bumps, and I was challenged at every turn, but that's what makes life great. In the end, I grew so much, had my best friends by my side, and I got the guy, so I think great is a perfect word.

"You got that right." Rachel kisses my cheek.

"Hey, that's my cheek." Everett leans in, grabbing my hips and spinning me so that we're dancing in each other's arms.

"That was my cheek first. These," Rachel slaps my butt, "are your cheeks."

I yelp, and her sauciness makes Scott, who grabs his girl-friend, laugh. Those two are made for each other. Damien scoops Bianca up, and the six of us slow dance in the vicinity of each other.

"I can't keep my hands off you," Everett growls in my ear as we sway.

Our sex life has been insane. Ever since we lost our virginities to each other in my basement, we're like crazed bunnies. Everett can't get enough, and sometimes I want to jump him when we're sitting at a dinner table with other people. Our need for each other, since we added sex to the mix, has only intensified tenfold.

And it doesn't help that tonight he's wearing a tuxedo that makes him look so freaking handsome, he should be on the cover of *GQ* or something.

"I have somewhere I want to take you." His stubble caresses my cheek.

"I thought we were taking the party bus to the shore house with everyone else."

It's tradition for Brentwick seniors to go to the Jersey Shore after prom and party in a rented house. I've been looking forward to this more than prom. One last ridiculous bash with my best friends.

"Oh, we're going to go party at the shore. Don't you worry your pretty little head. But, I thought tonight could be just about us."

Everett produces a room key from his pocket, waving it just in front of my nose.

"A hotel room on prom night? How cliché of you." I flutter my lashes.

"Well, it's not like anyone will be losing it. You know, since you've already let me inside you," he whispers in my ear.

I push at his chest, laughing, but he brings me back in close. His lips tickle my earlobe, his words winding in at a low octave. "I figured we could spend the next twelve hours in every position we haven't explored yet, before we're thrown in a house with your drunk high school friends. I want to devour you slowly, with no one else around."

Well, when he says it like *that*.

"Yes, you're inside me forever." My voice takes on a note of wistfulness.

"And you in me," he says, his deep voice switching from teasing to loving.

Everett and I have been attached on a deeper level for a long time. From the days of school kids, looking out for each other, to before he was deployed when we couldn't find the words or courage to admit our feelings. In a way, I'm glad we had the time to write all of those letters, because it made it easier to develop our connection with no teenage bullshit or physical intimacy in the way.

I used to feel like I didn't truly belong anywhere, even in the most familiar of places with the most familiar of people. Now, after all we've been through, we're better and stronger than we've ever been. Both individually, and definitely together.

And I know, that from here on out, wherever I go as long as Everett's with me, that will be my home.

He is my home.

EPILOGUE
EVERETT

Four Years Later

Coming off of an EMT shift, when you have difficult calls, is always exhausting.

But coming off of an all-night shift where you deal with two car accidents and a college student with alcohol poisoning ... that's a whole other level.

So when I pull up to my apartment and see a certain car parked outside, my heart warms and a smile spreads over my face. And I fall even more in love with her when I unlock the door and smell the scent of frying bacon.

"Woman, are you trying to get a ring out of me?" I call out and hear an answering laugh from the kitchen.

Kennedy walks out in yoga pants and a university logo sweatshirt, holding a plate stacked high with waffles. "Are you saying you want to marry me?"

She barely has time to put the plate down on my small kitchen table before I'm bear hugging her and lifting her off the ground. "You know I do."

In the last four years, our love has only grown stronger. To the point where I tell her daily that I'm going to get down on one knee. It's just a matter of time now, as Kennedy told me it has to be after graduation. She's always been a rule follower and getting engaged comes after college.

Although it doesn't mean she can't show up at my apartment to cook me breakfast after an all-nighter. Or sleep here three to four times a week.

She lives with her three best friends from college in a house just off campus. They all met freshman year in the dorms, and I'm glad she has people she's close with up here. I'm working a lot and have met a few buddies through my soccer league that I hang out with. I was adamant that she have her own college life, even though I followed her here. She deserved to have the full experience, and we're lucky everything has worked out so perfectly.

She graduates in two months, and then we're going to rent our first place together, wherever we end up. Right now, we're waiting back on some job offers Kennedy got, in three different cities. I'm letting her decide, because all I need is her, and a new adventure will be cool wherever it is. Her nursing program has been tough, but she's a star in her own right. I know that she'll help so many people, and her goal is to try to coordinate living in the same city as either Rachel or Bianca.

"Seriously, sit down. Food will be ready in two minutes." She kisses me quickly and then scurries back to the kitchen.

My place is small but functional, and it's been nice to have my own space that isn't my parents. I feel like a full-grown adult most days.

"Seriously, I love you. I have the best girlfriend ever. Sex and waffles after a long night at work? Perfection."

I passed my EMT course in New York about a month after we got here and immediately started picking up shifts at the local rescue squad. Throughout the course, I kept doubting myself that this was the job for me. Had I done it out of a moment of spontaneity? Was I really going to be able to help people?

My first night at the rescue squad by Kennedy's college, I saved a five-year-old boy from an overturned vehicle. I visited the hospital any time I could in that week where he was recovering from multiple injuries and still get a Christmas card from his family to this day. This job is the best decision, aside from letting Kennedy in, that I've ever made.

I was born for this. It's not the army where danger lurks around every corner. But it's enough that the chaos feeds my soul, and I'm doing real, *good* work. I still have nightmares from time to time, about my deployment overseas, but they're few and far between. I still see a therapist up here once a month and make sure to loop Kennedy in if it's a particularly hard day.

"Who said anything about sex?" She smirks as she comes in with the plate of bacon.

I sip from the coffee mug she already set down, though I shouldn't have caffeine if I'm about to go to bed.

"Well, you showed up in my apartment after work. And for any normal couple, that would be at night after a shift, meaning this is a full-blown booty call. So, show me that ass." I reach for her, tickling her side.

"Everett! Stop!" She laughs through huffed breaths.

God, she's gorgeous. And smart, and insanely patient. Kennedy is everything I'm not, and she makes me a better man.

And I wasn't kidding about wanting to marry her. She may make me wait until graduation, but that doesn't mean there isn't a diamond ring sitting in the drawer of my nightstand.

I can't wait to give it to her.

Do you want your **FREE** Carrie Aarons eBook?

All you have to do is **sign up for my newsletter**, and you'll immediately receive your free book!

ALSO BY CARRIE AARONS

ABOUT THE AUTHOR

Author of romance novels such as The Tenth Girl and Privileged, Carrie Aarons writes books that are just as swoon-worthy as they are sarcastic. A former journalist, she prefers the love stories of her imagination, and the athleisure dress code, much better.

When she isn't writing, Carrie is busy binging reality TV, having a love/hate relationship with cardio, and trying not to burn dinner. She's a Jersey girl living in Texas with her husband, daughter, son and Great Dane/Lab rescue.

Please join her readers group, Carrie's Charmers, to get the latest on new books, as well as talk about reality TV, wine and home decor.

You can also find Carrie at these places:
Website
Facebook
Instagram
Twitter
Amazon
Goodreads